Deception

Blue Moon Saloon
Book 5

by Anna Lowe

Twin Moon Press

Contents

Other books in this series

Blue Moon Saloon

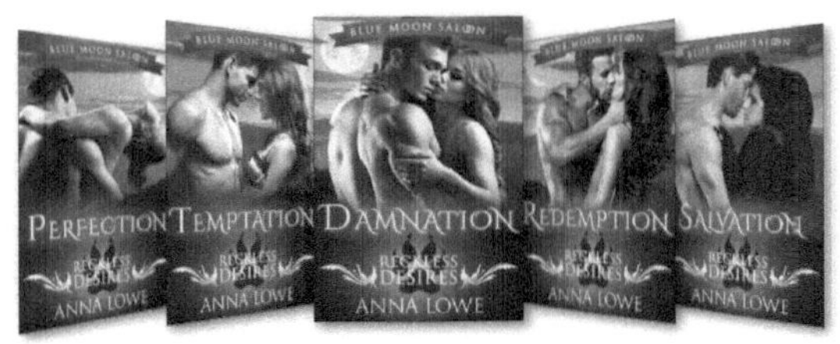

Perfection (a short story prequel)

Damnation (Book 1)

Temptation (Book 2)

Redemption (Book 3)

Salvation (Book 4)

Deception (Book 5)

Celebration (a holiday treat)

visit www.annalowebooks.com

Free Books

Get your free e-books now!

Sign up for my newsletter at *annalowebooks.com* to get three free books!

- *Desert Wolf*: Friend or Foe (Book 1.1 in the Twin Moon Ranch series)

- *Off the Charts* (the prequel to the Serendipity Adventure series)

- *Perfection* (the prequel to the Blue Moon Saloon series)

Chapter One

Summer hummed to the tune on the radio as she arranged the window display in the Quarter Moon Café. Little snowmen, miniature trees, and a tiny sled. She sprayed on more fake snow and looked up at the dusting of the real stuff that had fallen on the highest ridges around town overnight. She'd been in Arizona for a few weeks now, and the place never ceased to amaze her. The contrasts, the harsh beauty of it all. She loved the red rock outcrops, the rich green pines, and the pure white of the snow. It was so different from where she'd grown up along the Great Lakes, and yet she'd never felt more at home in her life. It was as if her heart had found a niche of exactly the right size and shape and wanted to settle in forever.

Which was a dangerously appealing thought, because she couldn't stay long. The shifters who ran the café and the neighboring saloon had been kind enough to take her in for the time being, but she knew she couldn't move in for good. Not after what she'd done. But where would she go next? Her home pack?

Her inner wolf snorted. *Never going there again.*

Where, then?

She had nowhere to turn. She'd been on the road for a long time with a pack she never wanted to return to, just like she never wanted to go back to being the person she'd once been. So naïve. So gullible. She was only twenty-five, but she felt a hundred years older and about a thousand wiser than she'd been just a few months ago.

So many mistakes. So many ugly memories. So many regrets.

She tipped her chin up and tried letting the sunshine cheer her up. She'd found a safe new place and a great group of people to live among — at least, for the time being. That's what counted most, right?

She stepped outside the café to check the display from the street, then went back in to adjust the reindeer pulling the sled.

"Perfect," she murmured, wishing she could arrange her life the way she arranged that display.

Well, it was almost perfect. Straw stars were the last part — straw stars just like the ones her grandmother used to decorate the Christmas tree with. That was one of the only memories she had of home that wasn't tainted by more recent events.

She sat down at a table by the window to make the stars, all the while inhaling the scent of breakfast. Jessica, her boss, was in the kitchen baking another batch of muffins, and the aroma of berries, vanilla, and cinnamon wafted through the room.

The bell over the door chimed merrily, and she looked up as a group of men filed in. As always, her heart skipped a beat in anticipation. Would Drew be among them?

"Morning, Summer." Luke, a wrangler from Seymour Ranch, tipped his cowboy hat.

"Having a good winter, Summer?" That was Mack, the jokester of the group.

"Hi, sweetheart. Got some of that coffee today?" Sam asked.

She greeted each with a genuine smile because they were all great guys. But when a fourth man crowded the doorway, her smile stretched cheek to cheek. Her whole face heated and flushed, and a boom like waves breaking over distant rocks registered in her ears.

Drew. Drew. Drew! her inner wolf cheered.

The other three men had come striding in like it was a second home, but Drew paused in the doorway. He did that every time, wiping his boots in a practiced right-left, right-left slide that said he'd been raised to do that at home. Then he pulled off his hat and stepped over the threshold.

Such a polite bear, her grandmother would have sighed.

He rubbed a thickly muscled shoulder against the doorframe in a territory-marking move that would have been a blatant challenge to the bears that owned the place if they weren't his cousins. And the way he did it screamed, *This place might not be mine, but it's mine to protect. Keep out, strangers. Don't even think about bringing trouble here.*

"Morning, Summer," he rumbled, locking eyes with her. His were a pale, gold-hued green, and they sparked with wonder when they took her in.

"Morning, Drew," she said, trying not to squeak.

A perfectly normal exchange of greetings, and yet it set off a dozen wild fantasies. Like hearing Drew utter those words while naked and sleepy in bed. Like replying and winding her leg around his as they lay skin to skin.

Morning, Summer, he'd say as she woke up, like it was the best morning ever because she was at his side.

Or maybe he'd just wake her with a quiet kiss and a touch — one that led to more touching and kissing and a long, unhurried session of making love.

Morning, Summer, he'd say when they dropped back onto the sheets, sweaty and satisfied. She'd rest her head on his chest — a chest so broad and so piled with muscle, she had dozens of options for exactly which subsection to try out — and run her hand down his thick, corded arms.

Summer cleared her throat and blinked. It was ridiculous, the way her body reacted to him. Her mind fluttered and took wing like a hysterical butterfly set loose in a meadow blooming with wild flowers.

Get yourself together, girl, she ordered herself.

But her inner wolf remained all dreamy, batting its eyes and wagging its tail.

A crush. It had to be a crush, right? And seriously, what woman wouldn't have a crush on a man like Drew? He was big, broad, and quiet. Honorable, too, like all bear shifters were. His close-cropped beard was thick, dark, and neatly trimmed, and she longed to tip forward and nuzzle it with her chin.

When he stepped closer, his eyes went a little hazy, too, as if he was thinking the same thing. The whole world started to fade away — the rumble of truck tires on the street, the quiet clink of silverware in the café, the murmurs of the other men. Everything receded to the far corner of her mind like a vague memory, and all she could see was Drew. All she could hear was the sharp intake of his breath as he looked at her, and all she could register was the rich, woodsy scent of him. She focused on his lips — thick, round lips that somehow fit perfectly on that edgy, masculine face, and she leaned forward even more. Their arms brushed, making blood rush through her veins.

Mate, her wolf murmured. *My destined mate.*

Mate, she swore she heard him think. *My destined mate.*

Then, *Bang!* The back door opened, and Jessica's cheery voice snapped her back to her heels.

"Morning, everyone!" her boss called, swinging a platter of muffins so fresh from the oven, they steamed.

Drew hastened a step back, and his eyes dropped to the floor. Summer gulped and blinked desperately, trying to find her focus again. Focus on something other than her favorite bear shifter, that is.

"Blueberry or apple?" Jessica held a platter of oven-fresh muffins up toward Drew.

"Um... uh..." He seemed as tongue-tied as Summer felt.

Luke reached in and helped himself. "Both, thanks. Can I get a coffee, too?"

"Make that two," Mack said.

"Three," Sam added.

Summer finally forced her feet into motion. "Coffee, coming right up." She stepped behind the counter to fill four mugs and inhaled deeply, hoping the rich scent would bring her back to her senses.

"Mind if we take these next door?" Sam asked as Jessica served more muffins.

Summer looked around. What was going on next door? And why did Jessica's face cloud? In fact, everyone went serious at the same time.

Then she remembered. Soren, the alpha of this unusual, mixed bear-wolf clan, had called a meeting with the wolves of Twin Moon Ranch. A meeting she hadn't wanted to think about because the subject was a vile enemy that had staged several attacks on the hard-working shifters she'd grown to love.

Worse, that enemy was the band of rogues she'd once worked for. The rogues she'd unwittingly assisted through so many heinous crimes.

Summer went stiff all over, remembering just who she was. Even if Drew felt anything for her, disgust would make him reject her in the end. How could he ever accept a she-wolf who'd taken part in crimes against his family? It was already a stretch for Jessica and the others to offer her shelter for a few weeks. Of course, that was probably in their best interest — that way, they could make sure Summer didn't have any tricks up her sleeve. She'd been working her ass off in the café and saloon, trying to prove she meant everything she'd said about her reluctant involvement with the Blue Blood rogues. But she knew she could never truly sweat away the guilt of what she'd been a part of. Her past would always be part of her. A black mark. A steel-barred cage. No matter where she went, no matter how hard she tried, she couldn't outrun her past.

And she certainly couldn't dream about taking a bear as a mate. The Blue Bloods had been defeated, but an idea was harder to eradicate than evil-hearted men. If any believers remained, they'd come after her and Drew to make an example of them.

Want my mate! her wolf wailed.

He couldn't, shouldn't be her mate. It wasn't meant to be.

Drew, she saw, was still standing nearby, looking at her. His face grew sad, and he dug his right heel against the floor tiles. Had he just remembered who she was, too?

"Sure, take the coffee with you," Jessica said, nodding toward the back. "We'll pick the mugs up later."

Luke, Mack, and Sam filed through the narrow corridor, and a second later, the rear door squeaked open.

"Coming, Drew?" one of them called back.

He went, watching her with dark, mournful eyes that refused to let go until the last possible second. His heavy steps echoed down the hall.

Mate, her wolf cried, seeing him go.

Summer closed her eyes, telling herself not to cry, too.

Chapter Two

Drew forced himself to follow the others down the dim hallway because if he didn't. . . well, who knew what kind of crazy stunt his bear might make him pull.

Like lunging for Summer and sweeping her into one of those bent-over-backward movie-poster kisses where the guy just couldn't get enough of the girl. Like throwing her over his shoulder and running her off to someplace down the road where they could be alone.

Alone. Good idea, his bear growled.

Yeah, him and her, alone. Talking. He desperately wished for someplace they could sit down to a cup of coffee — a coffee served by someone other than her — and talk and talk and talk. Not coming, not going. Just sitting and getting to know each other beyond *Good morning* and *Good night.*

Talk? his inner bear grumbled.

The beast had been all ears on the throwing-her-over-his-shoulder part, but that was about it. And that was the problem. The pull, the need, the craving for her was growing every day, and it scared the hell out of him to think what he might do.

Like take her somewhere private and get her naked, real fast? his bear suggested.

An image of Summer, gloriously naked and writhing in ecstasy under his body popped into his mind. Summer, with her blond hair flowing over her shoulders, her trim body begging for more. Her rich brown eyes fixed on his, her lips silently voicing her pleasure.

He gulped. Hard.

She wants it, too.

Yes, he'd seen the desire in her eyes. But he'd seen fear, there, too. Fear and longing and worry about things that pained him to even guess at. He wanted to make them all go away until there was nothing in her eyes but pure desire.

Okay, and maybe wonder. Love. Joy. All the things he felt for her in addition to the desperate physical need.

He'd only known her for a couple of weeks—

Nineteen days, eight hours, sixteen minutes, his bear threw in.

—and yet it felt like he'd thirsted after her for years. Her. Only her. Exactly her. Not any of the girls back home. Not Eileen, who was smart as anything and pretty, to boot. Not gorgeous Julie with her Hollywood smile. Not Bethany with the curves that brought all the guys to their knees.

None of them. Just Summer.

Need her. Want her. Must make her mine.

"You coming, or what?" Sam hurried him along.

He stepped into the blinding sunlight of the back lot and looped over to the rear door of the Blue Moon Saloon, the place adjacent to the café, where he ducked into darkness again. Which was fitting, given the mood of everyone in the room.

"All right already. Let's start," Soren Voss growled.

Soren, his distant cousin, the alpha of this clan. The man who'd requested backup from his black bear relatives on the East Coast. Soren and his fledgling shifter clan had survived numerous attacks in the past months, all of them staged by the Blue Blood rogues — an extremist group so staunchly against the mixing of shifter species that they were ready to kill any couple who dared cross species lines.

Soren and the others had felt that hate full force as a mixed clan of bears, wolves, and humans who'd been turned by their mates. Which made them all prime targets for the militant rogues. But they'd fought back, time and time again, and beaten the Blue Bloods so soundly, it was doubtful they would come back again.

Still, doubtful wasn't good enough, especially not for Soren. And Drew couldn't blame him. Soren had a young cub, a mate, and his extended family to protect. Not to mention a growing business to nurture, too.

"Todd and Anna killed the last of the Blue Bloods," a wolf called Kyle pointed out. He was one of several wolves present from Twin Moon Ranch — one of the most powerful shifter packs in the West.

"The question is, are those rogues gone for good?" Simon asked.

His words hung heavily over the room.

Drew kept quiet. One, because he was accustomed to the stricter traditions back home which only gave the elder generation the right to speak their minds. Two, because he really didn't know. He'd arrived in Arizona a week after that last attack, shortly after Soren requested backup.

We need loyal, quick-thinking bears ready to be vigilant against further attacks. Soren's message had said. *A big, capable fighter to help keep an eye on things here.*

When that message had been read aloud, every clan member's head turned to Drew, and a few hours later, he was on the road, heading west.

The third reason he didn't comment on the discussion was because Summer had stepped into the room with a tray of glasses, setting his mind and body on fire again. She moved with silent grace, distributing drinks in an unobtrusive way. Her hair shone in the dim light of the room, and it flowed over her shoulders in loose banana curls. The kind he'd like to wrap a finger in and wind around and around. The kind he'd like to wrap all his fingers around as he backed her against a wall and kissed her senseless while she made hungry mewling sounds.

He cleared his throat and sat straighter. Shit. Stupid bear, giving him bad ideas.

Good ideas. She'd like them, his bear insisted.

Summer walked past, and he sniffed deeply, inhaling her honeysuckle scent. A taste of heaven on earth.

Then she moved on, and a moment later, the back door swung open and closed. The second he felt her leave, his soul ached to see her again.

Man, what was wrong with him?

Mate, his bear growled. *She's my mate.*

He closed his eyes, trying to clear the words out of his mind.

Trust me, she's our fated mate. It's destiny.

Right. Trust fate. Everyone knew how fickle that mystical force could be.

"Damn rogues," Soren murmured, slamming a fist on the table.

Drew snapped his attention back to the room. Soren's mate, Sarah, put a hand on the clan leader's arm, calming him down. "I want to believe the rogues are gone. I want to believe we could stop looking over our shoulders and get on with our lives. I want to enjoy the holidays."

Every shifter in the room nodded in agreement.

"But..." She patted the baby sleeping in her arms and trailed off.

"But they could still be out there," Soren muttered with a murderous look on his face. "Who knows? There could be another Whyte. A new leader, ready to pick up their fucked-up crusade."

Everyone went silent, considering the possibilities.

Tina Hawthorne-Rivera, one the leading members of Twin Moon pack, spoke next. "The problem is not so much the Whytes but the sick idea they promoted and how to eradicate that."

Sarah shook her head sadly. "There will always be rogues with crazy ideas. What we need to concentrate on is whether they're regrouping or giving up. Whether they have a leader strong enough to plan another attack."

"Or a leader strong enough to show them a new way," Tina said.

"We should send up a contingent to their base in Utah," Luke suggested. "Wipe them out for good."

Drew sat up straighter. Summer had spent some time at that ranch in Utah. Hope Springs — that was the name of the place the Blue Blood rogues had taken over as a home base. Summer had been forced to work with the Blue Bloods until she'd fled. Was that why her eyes were so haunted? Was that the source of the massive guilt that seemed to weigh her down?

Tina shook her head. "We don't want to wage our own war. If we do, we're no better than them."

"We don't even know if they're still there or if they've moved on to some other place." Simon scratched his jaw.

The back door swung open, and Summer entered again, quiet as a mouse. Drew just about jumped out of his chair to see her again, but no one else seemed to pay much notice — not to Summer, nor to how loudly he was sure his heart was pounding. How could anyone overlook a woman like her?

It must have been her silent grace, her light-footed step. She moved like a dancer, and her hair swung in a silky wave. She brushed it back with the gesture he'd long since fallen in love with and scanned the room, distributing muffins and picking up empty glasses as she went. She had a gift for dodging attention and staying in the wings, it seemed. Was that what it took to help her survive her time with the rogues?

He looked at Soren, hoping his cousin would suggest driving to Utah and shaking information out of every man, woman, and child at the Blue Bloods' last known base. He sure as hell would be the first to volunteer. If the Blue Bloods were truly defeated, maybe Summer could move on. Maybe she could let herself laugh and love and live.

Laugh with me, his bear added. *Love me. Live with me.*

Any one of his buddies would fold into laughter if they heard his bear now. The bear who'd sworn he wasn't ready to settle down despite the plentitude of women offering him their all. He'd never felt ready for a mate and a home and kids. But the second he'd met Summer, the burning need for a mate had flipped on, and he couldn't find the off switch.

And not just any mate. Summer.

Summer, Summer, and Summer. Get it? his bear growled.

Yeah, he got it, all right. But what to do about it if Summer wasn't ready?

She came around his side of the room and placed a coffee by his hand. When she leaned close, her hair fell in a silky curtain, and he itched to brush it back. To taste her lips. To make the haunted expression fade from her eyes just long enough to have them shine at him.

When she slipped away again, he saw the shadows under her eyes. She looked a little ragged, probably from all the working hours she'd insisted on putting in at the saloon and café. Worse, Sarah said she'd heard Summer crying herself to sleep some nights.

He wanted to take hold of Summer's perfect hands and shake some sense into her. She thought she had to prove herself to the others? They'd long since accepted her. All she really needed was to accept herself.

Yes, she'd worked for the Blue Bloods. But she'd been forced to. She'd done everything in her power to thwart their plans, and she'd managed to save the shifter cubs the rogues had kidnapped. Why couldn't she move on?

"What we need is an insider," Kyle said. "Someone we can send to snoop around and see what the Blue Bloods are up to, if anything."

Summer stiffened at the mention of the rogue pack, and it took everything Drew had not to leap over and hug the anxiety out of her slight frame.

"But who? They'd see through us in a second." Sarah shook her head.

"Maybe we can get someone from another clan," Soren said.

"A wolf would be better," Tina said. "A wolf, like them. Maybe I can get someone from my sister's pack in California to help out."

"Are we really prepared to put someone in that kind of danger?" Sarah asked.

"If it's for the good of the pack," Tina said. "For the good of all shifters."

"I'll do it," Luke said, raising his hand.

Sam shook his head. "I know their type, believe me. I'll go."

Several others volunteered or murmured suggestions until a clear, determined voice spoke up, silencing everyone in the room.

"I'll go," Summer said, looking fiercer than he'd ever seen her before.

For a split second, he could hear the hum of the refrigerator behind the bar. It was that quiet. But a moment later, everyone broke into a hubbub, supporting or rejecting the idea.

"Too dangerous..."

"Too risky..."

"Well, she is one of them," someone else noted, making Summer wince.

She's not one of them, he wanted to roar. *She's one of us.*

The pained look in her eyes told him how much she wished for the same thing.

"Summer does know them," Tina admitted. "And they know her. She could pull it off."

Sarah nodded, too. "A deception. Summer can get closer to the rogues than any of us ever could."

Drew wanted to holler, *no, no, no!* But even he had to admit she was perfect. Just the way she'd ghosted through the room before proved it. For all her natural beauty, she had a way of slipping through space unnoticed. Of listening when she seemed to be tuned out.

But he noticed, damn it. He noticed her eyes go a tiny bit wider, showing a hint of fear. He noticed how she threw her shoulders back when she spoke, forcing herself to be brave. He noticed the tremble of her lips.

She took a deep breath and spoke so vehemently, no one could protest. "I'm the best one for the job. I'll do it."

I swear, her eyes added, blazing at everyone in the room.

∞∞∞∞

It all happened so quickly, Drew didn't have time to protest. Once the others jumped on the idea of Summer as their insider at Hope Springs, everyone rushed on to arrangements.

"I'll drive her to Utah," Luke said.

"She can hitchhike the last couple of miles to Hope Springs," Sam said.

Hitchhike? he nearly yelled.

"So no one sees any of us with her," Sam explained, and again, Summer winced.

13

"We'll give her two weeks to gather whatever information she can, then somehow report back..." Soren said, tapping his fingers on the tabletop.

Somehow?

Summer stood stiff as a statue, listening to them talk about her, not to her.

He wanted to bellow. Were they out of their minds? It was too dangerous. Too risky. Too rushed. Before he knew it, Tina had hurried Summer away to prepare to depart, concocting a cover story as she went. The back room of the saloon emptied quickly, and he stood there, clenching and reclenching his fists, ready to tear the place apart.

He grabbed Soren's arm before the bear alpha could lumber out of the room.

"This is crazy. Are you really going to let her go?"

Soren scraped a hand through his hair, and damn, he didn't look any surer about the idea than Drew was.

"I know it's crazy, but it makes sense, too. We killed all the rogues she was forced to work for. Whatever believers are left in Hope Springs don't know she resisted. She's perfect."

Well, of course, she was perfect. Just not in the way Soren meant.

"What if they figure it out?" Drew protested. "What if her cover is blown? They'd kill her on the spot."

Soren looked grim. "You got a better idea?"

He nodded immediately.

"I'll go."

Soren snorted. "Sure. Those crazy wolves would welcome my cousin into that fucked-up den of theirs. They'll trust you and spill all their secrets and all their plans. No problem."

He shook his head. "I could make up a story."

"Like what?"

"Like I've come on behalf of my clan. Katahdin clan, back home, I mean. A clan that's concerned about what their cousins in Arizona are up to."

Soren shoved him against the wall and fisted his shirt, looking ready to strangle him. "Is that what you're here for? I asked for help, and the clan sent me a goddamn spy?"

Drew locked his hands around his cousin's wrists and pushed back. "No. The clan sent me in good faith, just like you asked for. But yes, there are some elders who asked me to report back about what you're up to here."

"And what exactly were you planning to report?" Soren demanded, shaking with rage.

Drew stared his cousin right in the eye. "That you're doing your family proud. That those elders can take their old-fashioned bullshit and go straight to hell. You've built an amazing clan here. Everyone pulls together. Everyone cares. Everyone knows their job and does it well. It's everything a good clan should be."

Soren loosened his grip a little, and the aim of his glare went from Drew to a point on the floor. "Damn elders. I guess they're used to clans being made up of bears — and bears only."

Drew shrugged. "Time for them to get used to a new idea."

"Yeah." Soren exhaled and let him go with a belated pat to his crumpled shirt. "Sorry."

Drew scowled. Like he cared about his shirt. All he cared about was Summer. "Look, all I'm saying is they might buy that story and let me in."

"Summer is still better. It makes more sense."

"Then let me go with her. Let me protect her."

Soren shook his head immediately. "No way. They'd see through that in a minute."

"See through what?"

Soren scoffed. "It's obvious, man."

"What's obvious?"

"I see the way you look at her. She's your destined mate. You're crazy for her."

Drew pulled back, gaping. It was one thing to consider if Summer could be The One in private. But to have his cousin say it...

Still, he tried dismissing the idea. "I just met her."

Soren rolled his eyes. "With your destined mate, you just know. Your bear knows."

Told you so, the beast rumbled from inside.

Dang. Could she really be his mate?

Soren leaned closer. "No way can you go up there with her. They'd see through you in a second. She's better off without you. Trust me."

Better off without me? his bear bellowed, raging inside.

But shit, Soren had a point. The Blue Bloods were passionately against wolves mixing with other species. And he was a bear. If Soren had figured out how much he cared about Summer, the rogues might, too, and the whole plan would be blown.

"I'm sorry, man," Soren said. "You can't go. No way."

The words were meant to comfort him, but they were an order, too. Soren reinforced the message with a stern look before he turned and left the room.

And Drew? He stood there, shaking inside, wondering what the hell he could do.

A truck roared to life in the back lot, and someone shouted, "Summer, you ready to go?"

Drew hurried outside and gaped at Luke. "You're going already?"

"No time to waste, man. Those rogues could be plotting their next attack right now."

Jesus. He'd woken up that morning dreaming about Summer, thinking it would be a great day because he'd get to see her in and around the café. But the day was turning into a nightmare.

"But she's not ready," he protested.

I'm not ready. Not ready to let her go. He caught the thought before it slipped out. Shit. He'd never be ready to let her go.

"It's a six-hour drive, at least," Luke said. "She'll have time to get ready on the way."

"But...but..."

"Look, man. I know this is hard for you," Luke said, keeping his voice low.

Shit. Luke knew Summer was his mate, too? Did everyone know?

Then a thought struck him. Did Summer know?

If she did, she'd hidden it well. Of course, he'd seen her eyes sparkle for him. But she'd never sought him out alone or spoken to him one-on-one. What if she didn't feel the same way? Or worse, what if she'd internalized some of the nonsense the Blue Bloods had preached? He was a bear, and she was a wolf. He didn't have a problem with that, but maybe she did.

His bear chuffed, refusing to accept the idea.

Without thinking, he bolted up the stairs to the little apartment over the garage where Summer was staying. He'd been staying in one of the spare rooms above the saloon, and even the fact that his window faced the street and not Summer's side hadn't stopped him from dreaming about her every night.

Was she his mate? He told himself it didn't matter. He'd keep her safe even if she was someone else's mate. Even if it killed him.

"Summer." He grabbed the banister at the top of the stairs to keep from bursting into the room.

She was sitting on the couch, slumped over and shaking, and it wrecked him to see her like that.

She stood up quickly, trying to cover up her tears.

"Coming. I was just, um..."

You were just crying, he nearly said. It didn't matter that she'd brushed her cheeks quickly. He saw the shine on her skin.

His bear cried, too, and before he knew it, he d rushed to her side. And whoa — he hugged her, too, holding her close for the first time.

They stood in a tight knot, speechless, letting their hearts beat against each other. Desperately. Fearfully. But bit by bit, the pain and anger receded. Everything turned warm and fuzzy, and the outside world gradually receded to someplace miles away. He breathed in her scent and petted her hair.

Nice, his bear hummed. It was as silky as he thought. Silky and soft and so beautiful to behold, like the sight of her closing her eyes and hugging him back.

Then Luke beeped his horn outside, and fuck. The real world came blaring back.

Drew took a deep breath. Even if the occasion was all wrong, holding her felt so right.

"You don't have to go," he whispered, smoothing her hair. He tucked her head under his chin and squeezed, because fate was lurking nearby, ready to drag her away.

"I have to go," she sniffled. Her arms, though, wound around his waist and held him as hard as he held her.

Mate, his bear growled. *My mate.*

"Don't force yourself to do this, Summer. Don't. Everyone will understand."

She shook her head. "I have to go. Don't you see? I have to go."

The shake in her shoulders told him she was looking at her past. All those ghosts, grappling with her in a war he couldn't fight.

Trust, a deep, ancient voice whispered in the back of his mind. *You have to trust.*

Trust what? Trust Summer to some cruel fate? If that voice had come with a face, he would have been tempted to punch it. Everyone knew fate messed around with innocent souls, and God knew fate had messed around with Summer. She'd been through so much already.

Trust that she has to do this alone, the voice said, echoing in the darkest corners of his mind.

Hell, no. Why should Summer face the rogues alone?

It's not just the rogues she has to face, the voice murmured.

He sucked in his lips, not wanting to agree. But, damn. It was true. He had to force himself to let her go, didn't he?

Trust me, the voice said, fading away.

He hated the idea. Fate let so many terrible things happen. History was full of examples of suffering and loss. Every day, somebody suffered somewhere. Why the hell should he trust fate?

I don't want to let her go, his bear mourned.

But, shit. Maybe he had to.

She looked up at him with her chocolate brown eyes, making his breath catch. She wasn't looking at him. She was looking at his lips.

Kiss her, his bear whispered. *Kiss her good-bye.*

Kiss me, her eyes begged.

He tipped his head down as she tipped hers up, and just like that, they connected. Really connected, like he'd never felt before. Not just by lips that moved gently, mournfully over each other. They were connected in the soul. He felt it in the tingle of his blood, the warmth that seeped into his veins.

Mate! his bear sang. *My mate.*

He pulled her even closer, deepening the kiss, tasting her when she opened her mouth. He treasured each exquisite sensation as it exploded in his mind. The way her tongue slipped over his lips. The perfect curve of her teeth. The way her body molded to his. She was so much slighter than him, and yet it was as if she'd been carved to fit in his arms. Or maybe he'd been carved to fit around her. Whatever. Energy pulsed between them, crackling like a fire kindled in a hearth. She cupped his face without letting go of the kiss, inhaling him as desperately as he held her.

She tasted so good. She felt so warm. Her scent overwhelmed him — the true scent of summer, when everything was alive and flourishing and bright.

Then the horn beeped again, and they broke apart.

He cursed under his breath. But Summer's eyes fluttered shut again, and she leaned back in.

All mine, his bear growled. *My mate.*

The voice of warning tut-tutted in the back of his mind.

It would have been so easy to get lost in that kiss. To forget all about good-bye and let his hands explore. To touch her, to make her feel good. To rub his bare skin over hers while she wrapped her legs around him.

Getting naked with her was all too easy to imagine, because he'd dreamed it a dozen times already. Peeling her clothes off, exploring what she liked. Showing her what he liked, too, and discovering new pleasures together. Feeling her trust him...

Trust. There it was again. A reminder of the reality facing them both. Summer didn't need him to hold her back. She needed him to let her go.

He took a deep breath and held her tight for one second longer, pouring confidence and power from his body to hers. And finally, reluctantly, he released her.

They both gulped for a moment, gazing into each other's eyes without saying a word.

"I didn't want our first kiss to be a good-bye," she whispered, making him smile.

Our first kiss. So he hadn't been the only one thinking about it. He liked that. He liked the way she ran her hands down his chest, too.

"It won't be the last one. I promise," he said. And damn, his voice had gone all husky on him.

She caught her lip between her teeth and stared at him, and all the sorrow he'd felt earlier welled up again. He beat it back for her sake.

"I promise," he said, and that time, his voice was hard, resolute.

I promise, his bear echoed inside.

The truck's horn blew outside. Drew steeled himself not to let the pain show as Summer pulled slowly away from him, moving to the stairs.

"You really promise?" she asked, looking so valiant yet so afraid.

And shit, he was afraid, too. Like never in his life before. What if he couldn't keep his promise? What if fate didn't let him?

He shook the fear out of his head — that wouldn't help her — and shoved certainty at her in waves. "I promise. I swear on my life."

Chapter Three

One week later...

Summer shivered and hurried across the yard, looking up at a wintery Utah sky. God, she missed Arizona and the Blue Moon Saloon. She missed her room in the apartment over the garage.

And boy, did she miss Drew.

She missed his low, rumbly voice. His big bulk filling up the door. The sound of him carefully wiping his boots on the mat. She missed his rich, woodsy scent and warmth.

Here, she was cold and alone. So terribly alone

She'd been in Hope Springs for a week now, and she was still on edge. The constant deception, the sidelong looks she received — they made her shiver as much as the frigid temperatures in the high-altitude desert.

The place would have been pretty if... She stopped herself there. It *was* a pretty place. The landscape, at least. Hope Springs homestead backed onto a huge step of the Colorado Plateau, where millions of years of earth's history showed in a rainbow of rock layers. A light dusting of snow was all the more brilliant against the reds, oranges, and browns of the exposed earth. But the haphazard collection of run-down trailer homes seemed to have been discarded rather than arranged as a community. It was hard to tell abandoned buildings from the occupied ones. Paint was peeling, mosquito netting sagging, and no one made an attempt to beautify the area. No flowers, no tidy porches, no cheerful colors.

When she'd first stepped foot on the place, she'd been tempted to turn around, head back to Arizona, and report that the Blue Bloods were defeated, once and for all. But there was an undercurrent to the scrappy little settlement of seventy-plus shifters. An unsettled feeling that made the back of her neck itch. Maybe the hatemongers were still at work here. Maybe the danger wasn't in the past.

"Summer!"

She halted in her tracks. Of all the things that made her shiver in Utah, none beat the nasal tone of Gretchen's voice. She turned and forced a neutral look over her face. "Hello."

"Come on over, honey," the fifty-something woman called.

The *honey* rippled with some subtext she was afraid to read into, and *come on over* was a command. When Gretchen patted the crooked seat beside her, Summer's instincts screamed at her to turn and run.

Gretchen Walker, née Whyte. Sister of Victor and Emmett Whyte — the men who'd taken the Blue Blood organization from a loose band of fist-shakers to a marauding gang of murderers. Victor and Emmett had been killed in attacks they'd staged on the Blue Moon Saloon, which served them right. But Gretchen...

Summer still wasn't sure of the woman's role in the rogue pack, but she didn't have a good feeling about it.

"You settling in well?" Gretchen studied her with that piercing look, and her nostrils flared.

That was the hardest part of going undercover at Hope Springs. Wolf shifters like Gretchen were sensitive to the slightest change in facial expression, and they could sniff out a person's emotions. Like fear. Like shame. Like disgust. Summer couldn't let her guard down for a second.

The problem was, lies didn't come naturally to her, and neither did deception. But hers was a life-or-death mission. The peaceful existence of countless shifters was at stake.

Plus, she could do *unremarkable* and *emotionless* like a champ. She'd had to for the awful months she'd been dragged along by the rogues. In fact, she'd unconsciously taken on that role for most of her life. No one noticed her moods. Hell, they rarely noticed her presence.

Drew noticed, her wolf murmured. *He didn't miss a thing.*

She locked the thought away in the back of her mind. She couldn't afford to let the hunky bear sneak into her thoughts now.

"Well, I'm still getting used to it all," she said. The closer she stuck to the truth, the better her chances of going undetected. "Thanks for asking. How are you?"

She bit back a scowl, hoping Gretchen wouldn't go into another tirade over the death of her brothers.

Gretchen sighed. "Good thing I have my boys. They keep me going."

The "boys" were four hulking, dim-witted wolf shifters close to Summer's age who'd been brought up on a gospel of hate. At first, she'd worried they might become the next generation of extremists. But without the strong leadership of a Victor or Emmett Whyte, Gretchen's sons were lost, rudderless. The most they got up to was drinking, polishing their rifles, and taking potshots at any jackrabbit unlucky enough to bounce through their sights.

No, Gretchen's sons weren't the men Summer worried about. She worried about the Emmett Whyte look-alike coming toward her now.

Her inner wolf growled, and she forced herself not to bare her teeth.

"Hello, Mett. Care to join us?" Gretchen called.

The man went by Mett, but Summer knew who he really was. Emmett Junior — son of the Blue Blood leader she despised.

"Hiya, Aunt Gretchen." The tobacco he chewed showed with every lazy syllable. When his eyes moved to Summer, they slid up and down her body in a slow, greedy path. "Hiya, Summer."

"Hi," she forced the word through gritted teeth.

"You doing good?" he asked, shifting the wad of tobacco from side to side.

She felt sick to her stomach, but she could hardly say that. "Fine."

"You thought about what I asked you before?"

Her fingers curled so tightly, her nails bit into her palms. Mett had come up to her soon after she'd arrived, asking her about his father's death.

Those no-good bear shifters did it, right? he'd all but spat.

Which made it pretty damn clear where Mett stood in terms of the purity issue.

He looked just like his father. He spoke in hateful tirades just like his father. He cursed any shifter who crossed species lines, just like his father. But that wasn't the worst of it. Mett seemed to think she'd been a volunteer on Emmett Whyte's murderous campaigns instead of a reluctant accessory to his crimes. Mett had even slung an arm over her shoulders, breathed tobacco in her ear, and tried to comfort her.

I know you did your best to help him.

She'd just about retched. She'd done her best to get away, but she couldn't exactly say that.

Mett made her sick. Her own past made her sick.

She'd tried wiggling away from him, but his hold only grew tighter.

Listen, I was thinking, Summ, he'd said next.

She hated when people shortened her name.

You and me...

As he went on, she went still as a stone.

We'd be perfect together. We can carry on my dad's work. Make sure shifters keep their species pure. He'd grinned madly at that point. *And just think. I bet we'd make some beautiful, pure-blooded pups together.* His hand had slid from her back to her ribs, closing in on the side of her breast.

She had slapped his hand and stepped away as his grin turned to a glare.

Shit. She'd managed to cover up quickly, thank goodness.

Um, sorry, she'd said, remembering her mission. *I guess I'm still, um...*

She fumbled for words for a second. Disgusted? Sickened? Appalled by what his father had done?

Still mourning? Mett had filled in, calming again. The man was as Dr. Jekyll-Mr. Hyde as his father had been. *Yeah.*

I miss him, too. But think about it, Summ. Think of everything I could do for you.

Oh, she'd thought about it, all right. And the prospect turned her stomach every time.

A fly buzzed past while Mett and Gretchen waited for her answer.

"I guess I'm still getting settled in," she mumbled, hoping it came off as meek instead of disgusted.

"Well, don't you worry your pretty little head about things." Mett grinned. "I got it all figured out."

His words echoed in her mind, and she tasted bile. *Don't worry your pretty little head. . .*

For so many years, she'd done just that. Back in her home pack in Minnesota, she'd worked in a diner and done some babysitting on the side. Pack politics didn't interest her, so she'd never really paid attention to those goings-on.

She couldn't remember when she'd heard the first grumbled tirades against shifters who crossed species lines. It sounded reasonable enough to her. Wolves should stick with wolves, panthers should stick with panthers, and so on. Live and let live, she figured.

God, how naïve she'd been.

It had all seemed so distant, so unrelated to her. But then Victor Whyte started preaching about purity of blood lines and the imminent decline of wolf shifters. From that point on, everything changed. A slow, gradual change she didn't see coming until it was too late. Hardly anyone raised a voice to question Whyte's rhetoric, and those who did — well, they were quickly put in their place. Eventually, Victor headed west on what he called a crusade, and most people just exhaled. Then Emmett Whyte started making noises, too, and her stepfather, Clark, had nodded with every hate-filled sentiment.

She trembled, remembering the night Clark had shaken her out of bed to follow Emmett and the others.

"Shh! Keep quiet!" Clark had hissed.

She went without protest, because she'd been brought up to follow her leaders and keep her mouth shut.

Both those things became harder and harder to do as time went on. At first, Emmett, Clark, and the others left her behind in whatever place they picked as a base while they went out "preaching," as they called it. Later, they started using her to feel out their targets. At the time, she'd thought all she was doing was placing a few calls or asking questions around a neighborhood. Harmless little things, part of the preparation for the "negotiations" Emmett and the others had been tasked to carry out.

Or so they claimed.

But then Emmett, Clark, and the others started coming back dirty and disheveled. Sometimes, they were bloody from fighting. Even then, she didn't ask questions, because it wasn't her place. And when her stepfather died in an attack, she'd hated the shifters that did that to him until Emmett explained.

Clark died for our cause, fighting those who are unpure.

When she finally figured it all out, she'd been shocked. She'd been helping to hunt down mixed shifter couples. She'd arranged ambushes without even realizing it.

But...but... she'd stammered. *You said you're negotiating.*

Don't be ridiculous, child. Emmett dismissed her, as he always did.

But you're killing them!

Of course, we're killing them! he'd snarled in her face. *They are unpure! They weaken us all!*

She wanted no part of that sick crusade, but Emmett wouldn't let her go. The day she finally worked up the nerve to run for the hills, she'd caught the sound of wailing babies and arguing men.

Kill them, Emmett was saying. *Just kill them.*

She'd stopped dead in her tracks. Emmett was going to kill innocent children?

Wait! She had rushed over and found the men clustered around two petrified cubs torn from their dead mother's side.

What are you doing? She'd clutched the children to her body, protecting them instinctively. *How sick are you?*

They are unpure, Emmett replied in a horrifyingly emotionless tone. *They die.*

He might have killed her, too, if her desperation hadn't fueled a crazy plan.

Don't kill them! Keep them alive.

Somehow, she managed to convince Emmett to spare the cubs — for a little while. If Emmett hadn't gotten sidetracked into hunting down the wolves and bears of the Blue Moon Saloon, who knows what might have happened?

The Blue Moon Saloon shifters had killed Emmett and his gang then taken the babies under their wing. Fay and Ben had a good home now, up in Montana with Soren's cousin, Todd, and his mate, Anna. Not only did the Blue Moon clan save the babies — they saved Summer, too, giving her a place to work and live.

But hell, here she was, back in a den of wolves. Who was an enemy? Who might be an ally?

Sometimes, she wanted to fold into a ball and cry to go home. But there'd be no home for her, no peace if she didn't see this through.

She masked her roiling emotions and faced Mett with a neutral expression. He looked hopeful, as if she was likely to squeal, *Yes! I'd love to be your mate, you racist, murdering pig.*

"I guess I still need more time to clear my head," she said.

Gretchen scowled. And the creases on her forehead folded even more deeply when a second man joined them. A tall, blond wolf shifter whose presence made Mett take a step back.

"Hello, Thomas," Gretchen murmured, not at all pleased.

He stepped up, tipping his hat and nodding to both women. "Hello."

Every woman in Hope Springs swooned over Thomas. He had the chiseled good looks of a daytime soap opera star, the build of a champion quarterback, and a ready, genuine smile. Like Summer, he was a newcomer to the settlement, and he seemed a perfect gentleman in every way. Apparently, he was the second son of a powerful alpha from somewhere up north.

A shifter coming into his prime and ready to lead a pack of his own.

And like Mett, Thomas' eyes shone a little brighter when he looked at her.

Shit. Shit, shit, shit. What was it about falling in love for the first time — in love with Drew, that is — that made her a magnet for other men? It was as if Drew had reached into her heart and turned on a light that everyone could see.

If she could have turned tail and run back to Arizona, she'd have done it there and then. But she couldn't. She had to stay and figure out what direction this leaderless pack seemed to be taking, how much of a threat they still were.

"If you'll excuse us..." Thomas murmured to Mett, taking Summer by the arm and leading her away.

She followed, if only to escape the clutches of Gretchen and Mett, and shot a sidelong glance at Thomas. If Mett worried her with his sick beliefs, Thomas worried her with his charisma and inborn strength. The man was an alpha through and through. If he was to take over the leadership of this pack, everyone would follow like blind sheep, exactly as she once had. And who knew how radical his beliefs were?

She watched Thomas surreptitiously. Was he capable of horrors like those perpetuated by the Whytes?

"How does it feel to be back home?" Thomas asked.

Home? Hope Springs wasn't home. The Blue Moon Saloon was. She'd only spent a short time in Hope Springs — another brief stop before Emmett and his gang set off again on their crazy quest.

"I guess I'm still trying to figure out where home is," she said truthfully.

Gretchen appeared out of nowhere and patted Summer's arm with her long, bony fingers. "We'll rebuild, honey. One step at a time."

Exactly what she was afraid of. She looked at Thomas, wondering where he stood.

Thomas murmured in agreement. "One step at a time."

Man, was he impossible to read.

Three pickups drove into the compound and parked by the ramshackle barn used as a meeting house. Summer watched as several shifters she didn't recognize exited their vehicles.

"Time to get started," Thomas said. His nostrils flared, and his shoulders grew stiff.

"Started?" Summer asked.

He nodded toward the barn. "The meeting. Why don't you come?"

She froze and stared at the barn. Community meetings in this pack were a men-only thing. Only a select few women attended — like Gretchen, of course. Summer had never been to a meeting, and with the Whytes in charge, she'd never considered asking to attend.

"Please come," Thomas said in a softer voice. "I'd like you to come."

His eyes were softer, too, and for a second, she thought she caught a whiff of the telltale scent of a wolf's arousal.

Her stomach flipped. Shit. Thomas couldn't be interested in her *that* way, could he? She didn't want the attention or the complication.

I just want Drew, her wolf cried.

Gretchen scowled in open disapproval.

"Sure," Summer said, following Thomas. What choice did she have? "That would be great."

The scratch of hurried footsteps behind her said Gretchen was coming, too, and when Thomas held the door open for her, Gretchen shouldered through first.

Summer sighed. That woman was as into hierarchy as the worst of the men.

Thomas winked at her, and her gut roiled. What if her whole plan went wrong and Thomas forced her to help in more attacks? After all, Emmett and Victor Whyte had been considered charming in their day.

She glanced over at Mett and hid a frown. Obviously, charm could skip generations, too.

When Thomas touched her arm, she wanted to run. Instead, she took a deep breath and followed him. But when he took a place at the front, she slipped around behind the crowd and tried melting into the woodwork as she scrutinized every face.

There were a dozen locals there already, most of them older men who'd gone along with the Whytes' sick dream without actually participating in any attacks — at least, as far as she knew. The newcomers seemed to have come separately, and more were still filing in. Wolf shifters, all of them. The men shook hands and leaned in close to each other in private conversation.

Can't wait to go kill some more innocent shifters, she imagined one saying to another. Or was the man saying, *It's about time we dissolved this crazy-ass pack?*

The strongest alphas — those who might vie for leadership of this pack — were easy to spot. They were the ones exuding testosterone with every bold step, every sidelong glance that put others in their place. As more and more shifters arrived, she gaped. How did she miss that this meeting was going to take place?

She shook her head at herself. Of course, there'd be a meeting sooner or later. And of course, no one would have told her about it because it wasn't her place. She looked up a second later, determined not to slip into her old ways. She'd tune in to every word, analyze every gesture.

"All right, let's begin." One of the older locals called the meeting to order. "We're here for nominations for leadership of the Blue Blood pack."

It sounded so civilized, though she suspected it would end in the usual bloody mess. Wolves didn't just run for candidacy. They fought to the death.

Everyone's eyes slid to two men: Thomas and a scarred old wolf from somewhere farther west. After a weighty silence, they both stepped forward and glared at each other.

"I'm for Thomas," someone to her right whispered to a friend.

"I'm for Dryver," the other said. "He's older. More experienced. He already leads his own pack. We could join them."

Summer scribbled notes on her mental notepad. The problem was, neither Thomas nor Dryver was transparent enough to understand. Well, no alpha ever was. Even when the crowd started lobbing questions at the men, they both danced around the issue of continuing the so-called crusade against unpure shifters.

"Who are you for?" Mett slid up beside her and whispered in her ear.

She flinched. "Whoever's the better leader, I guess."

That sounded vague enough, didn't it? Vague and air-headed, like she'd used to be. But inside, she considered what her true answer might be. Thomas? Dryver? Neither?

Summer took a long, deep breath, trying to memorize which person raised which point. Many of the men in the crowd seemed to want nothing more than peace and prosperity, but a few seemed sympathetic to the Whytes' cause as they threw question after question at Thomas and Dryver.

"What qualifies you to lead this pack?" That question came in various forms, and both candidates parried it easily.

"What would you do about this pack's debt?' someone asked as the questioning went on and on.

"What do you think this pack needs most?" Summer spoke up at a pause.

A dozen surprised heads turned, none more disapproving than Gretchen's tightly drawn face.

I don't remember you speaking up in meetings before, dear, her drop-dead expression said.

I didn't think for myself before, Summer wanted to say.

"Stability. Time to recover," Thomas said immediately. "Strong leadership."

Dryver nodded and shot out an equally neutral reply. "Firm rules and a common goal."

She was about to ask what that goal might be when the door swung open and a ray of sunlight sliced into the room. Every head in the room turned, and a pregnant pause ensued — the kind that announced the entrance of a powerful alpha who could change everything. From the shocked look on some faces, she half expected Ty Hawthorne, the imposing leader of Twin Moon pack, to stride into the room.

Whoever it was took a long time to enter. A whisper went through the crowd, but she didn't catch the words. She was too busy focusing on a sound. The sound of feet wiping on a doormat.

Right, left. Right, left.

Her heart skipped.

A burly figure stepped slowly over the threshold, rubbing a thickly muscled shoulder against the doorframe in a bold move that said, *I might not own this place, but I am not a man to be fucked with.*

A rumble went through the wolves gathered there as they sniffed his oaky scent.

Drew, her wolf cried. *Drew!*

"Ho-ly shit," someone exclaimed.

"A bear? Who the hell invited a bear?" another person whispered.

Drew looked around slowly as if to say, *Go ahead and challenge me.* No one did. They just stared dumbly.

She stared, because it was Drew, but it wasn't Drew. This was a rougher, tougher, *rawer* version of the man she'd kissed. Meaner, almost. All the gentleness had gone out of him, and he was all warrior, all power.

Ho-ly shit was right. Back at Blue Moon Saloon, he'd never shown his full strength. Perhaps he hadn't had the occasion to. But now...

"Man, oh, man. Let's not piss him off," someone whispered.

"To whom do we owe the pleasure?" Thomas said in a carefully neutral voice. He stretched to his full height and turned on his alpha wolf glare that Drew met, watt for watt.

"Pleasure's all mine," Drew said. His deep voice resonated throughout the room.

"What the hell do you want here?" Dryver barked in open challenge.

Summer held her breath, watching Drew's fists clench.

Chapter Four

Drew paused, taking in his surroundings. The room crackled with anticipation like a thunderstorm that had dead-ended in a box canyon. Fear, hate, and suspicion swirled around the room, and a rush of whispers reached his sensitive ears.

"A bear! A bear!"

What, had they never seen a bear shifter before?

"Don't tell me he's one of those no-good Vosses," someone else growled.

Just a distant relative, but hell, yeah. He was all on board with his cousins. The problem would be hiding that from this ugly crowd.

That, and hiding his attraction to Summer. Pulling this deception off. He could scent her from across the room, and his bear was screaming to run over and smother her in a kiss.

Inside, his bear paced, but on the outside, he battled to keep perfectly still. Soren had been right to keep him from following Summer, saying it was much too obvious that he was interested in the she-wolf.

Interested? He was damn near obsessed. He'd barely slept over the past week, and the few hours he'd caught were filled with dreams of Summer smiling at him or nightmares of her screaming for help. He'd even charged out of bed one night, determined to race to her side, but Soren convinced him to turn back, saying Summer was safer without anyone there to give her true mission away.

But then an anonymous message had reached the Blue Moon Saloon, and that changed everything.

I don't fucking believe it, Soren had muttered, reading the email that came in from an account they couldn't identify.

Inside man willing to work with you to keep Blue Bloods under control, the message said. *There's been enough violence. Might need your support. Are you with me?*

The writer had signed with an X. Nothing more.

Could be a trick, Soren said.

Could be the real thing, Simon shot back.

Can't trust anyone, Drew had thrown in.

Soren and Simon had deliberated it with the wolves of Twin Moon Ranch and finally decided to send Drew to Hope Springs while they tried getting more information out of the author of that note.

If this guy is legit, we don't need Summer up there, Soren had said, and Drew had just about exploded out of the saloon in his rush to depart. But Soren wasn't finished. *If they're trying to con us, Summer could be in more danger than we thought.*

Which was when he really did explode out of the saloon and hit the road. And now that he'd finally made it, all the emotions Summer triggered hammered him at once. Love. Lust. Joy. Fear. It took everything he had not to swivel in her direction and reveal all that. Hell, it took everything he had to resist running over and pulling her into his arms.

He took a deep breath and ordered himself not to betray his emotions. A good thing he had some practice hibernating — it helped him force his heartbeat to a crawl. And hell, he'd never had to do that quite as much as right now. His pulse was thumping, his nerves twitching. His bear wanted to maul every wolf in sight, grab Summer, and steal her away from this bad place. Every shifter pack suspected outsiders, but these wolves had knives in their eyes. How had Summer survived a week here?

"What the hell do you want here?" a man barked.

Drew ignored the scarred old wolf and kept his eyes on the younger, fair-haired one. Every instinct told him that was the wolf to watch out for. That one was smarter, subtler, and much harder to read. Was it he who sent the message to Soren?

Drew doubted it. The guy seemed cocky as hell — not the kind to ask for outside help. Was it that older woman sitting to one side, listening intently? She looked capable of anything — like selling out her own pack or faking a call for help. Impossible to tell which. The three bearded men looking at him closely from the front row looked old and weary before their time. Could they have sent the message?

Jesus, was there anyone here he could trust?

No one. Well, apart from Summer.

He channeled all the power of his bear clan into a fierce look and made a slow sweep of the barn, studying every face. He forced his eyes to run smoothly past Summer, but boy, was that hard. She looked drawn and thin — thinner than before. He ached to take her home and feed her berry pancakes covered in honey. His favorite treat. Could it be hers, too?

He buried the thought in the back of his mind and trained all his focus on the two alphas up front. To whom did they owe the pleasure?

"Drew Kovacs of the Katahdin clan," he said, letting a hint of warning fill his voice.

"Powerful East Coast bear clan," someone murmured.

His chest puffed out a bit. Damn right.

"Thomas Miller," the blond guy said. He didn't mention a pack, which meant he'd either been kicked out of his former pack — unlikely, given that obvious strength — or was the second or third son of a powerful alpha who wanted to run his own pack. The dangerous kind — accustomed to privilege and hungry for power.

"Dryver," the old guy said next. "Of Deer Mountain pack. You any relation to those Voss bears?"

Every shifter in the room leaned forward, and more than one set of claws was unsheathed. He could sense them sliding silently out as the wolves barely held back.

A moment of truth. What he said next would make or break his entire mission.

"Cousin," he admitted.

Alarmed voices broke out around the room, but one look from Thomas silenced them. Yep, he was definitely the wolf to watch out for here.

Drew had rehearsed his lines a hundred times on his way north, so they came easily now.

"My clan is concerned about the behavior of our relations out West."

That was near enough the truth. There were plenty of bears at home who disapproved of his cousins breaking tradition and taking mates who weren't bears. The disapproval was nowhere near the murderous knee-jerk reaction of these killer wolves, though. More like a little headshaking among the older bears. But he didn't have to share those details.

"They sent me out to talk to the bears who run the Blue Moon clan." That was mostly true, too.

"It's not a clan. It's a disgrace!" someone shouted.

He ignored the source and focused solely on the reaction of the two alphas before him. Were they as radical as he feared?

Dryver bared his teeth at the man who'd called out — more in a *you should be seen and not heard* gesture than *I disagree with your stance* disapproval.

"And you came here to. . . ?" Thomas leveled a cool gaze at Drew, still impossible to read. Funny how every look, every question felt like a trap. An ugly, steel-jawed bear trap.

I came here to get my mate out of this sick place, his bear wanted to roar. *To take her home and tell her just how I feel about her.*

"The leaders of my clan sent me here to report back on the activities of the Blue Bloods. Nothing more." He kept his voice carefully neutral, just like his choice of words.

Thomas tilted his head in a *that can be interpreted in more ways than one* gesture, which was exactly what Drew intended. His words could be interpreted to mean that the Katahdin pack was considering supporting the Blue Bloods in their quest for purity. Which was utter bullshit, but Thomas didn't know that. Second, his careful word choice prevented the scent of a lie from slipping out, because the statement was true, in a way. Soren — a member of his clan, at least in the extended sense — really had sent him to Utah for information.

And to maim, rip apart, or kill any wolf who threatens my mate while I'm at it, his bear added.

Even Drew could smell the warning that wafted off his own shoulders with that thought, but that was fine. Let the wolves see him bristle. Let them stay on their toes.

"To report." Thomas echoed his words, arching his eyebrows in a question.

A question Drew sure as hell wasn't going to field right now. The less he said, the longer he could pull off his ruse.

All I want is my mate. Get her to safety. Make her mine, his bear growled.

Yeah, well. He wanted that, too, but there was more to the situation than just him and Summer. The future of all shifters was at a tipping point.

Grizzled old Dryver folded his thick arms and glared at him. "That is our pack's business, not yours."

"Whose pack?" Drew retorted, looking between the two men before him to make his point. Who would lead the Blue Bloods, and what would his agenda be?

The old man scowled. "That will be decided soon."

Soon could never be soon enough for him — and Summer felt the same. He could feel her impatience, even from this distance. The tension, too, that he wanted to massage out of her shoulders. The anxiety about what might transpire next.

He kept his arms away from his sides just in case, because the crowd had broken into dozens of separate conversations — all of them heated. A brawl might erupt any minute, and he'd better be prepared to fight his way to Summer and help her escape.

But Thomas and Dryver managed to get the place settled down again — Thomas with seething looks and no noise whatsoever, Dryver with harsh shouts. Drew would put his money on Thomas winning the position of alpha. That was the easy part. The hard part was figuring out what Thomas would do next. Would he lead the pack into a new era of live and let live, or would he set off a shifter war?

"Order! Order!" Dryver pounded his fist on a table. Between that and Thomas' glare, the place settled down.

"The alpha of this pack will tell you what you can report to your clan, bear," Dryver said. His voice dripped scorn at the word *bear*.

"Yes," Thomas murmured. "He will."

"That question will be settled tonight," Dryver replied, giving Thomas the evil eye.

The crowd broke into chatter again. "A fight! A fight!"

Drew looked around. Shit. He'd never seen shifters so eager for blood.

"Tonight." Thomas nodded.

The gauntlet had been thrown down; the challenge accepted. Everyone started jabbering at the same time, and all the focus was on the two candidates for alpha. The two who would duel, wolf style, for leadership of this pack.

Drew risked a glance at Summer. Every wolf in a fifty-mile radius would attend the fight, which meant...

Summer's warm brown eyes sparkled as she caught the gist of his thoughts.

If everyone was glued to the fight, no one would notice the absence of one quiet she-wolf and one brawny bear.

His inner beast all but rubbed his paws together in anticipation.

He turned away from Summer before anyone could notice and faked a bored look that said, *Wolves. Such heathen creatures. Nothing like bears.*

Which was partially true. Bears deliberated carefully, while wolves reacted from the gut. Bears proceeded with caution, not hot heads.

He thought of Summer, and his blood rushed. Bears knew the meaning of passion, though, in the things that counted most. Like honor. Like duty. Like love.

He'd serve his clan, and he'd do whatever it took to keep his mate safe. But the question was, could he do both?

Trust me, a voice deep in his mind said. *When the time comes, trust me.*

He shook his head. There it was again. The voice of fate. He wanted to snort. No way was he trusting anyone but himself.

"You, bear, have been heard," Thomas said when the room quieted down again. "The alpha of this pack will meet with you tomorrow." He made a subtle motion toward his own chest.

"Yes." Dryver scowled. "He will."

Drew looked over both candidates. Which of them would be dead by morning? Thomas was a wolf in his prime, but the experience of a veteran like Dryver was not to be discounted.

"Tonight," Dryver said, glaring at Thomas.

"Tonight," Thomas barked back.

They meant the fight, of course. But when Drew reached his thoughts out to Summer, he had an entirely different meaning in mind.

Tonight, he thought, hoping she might read his thoughts.

Tonight. A faint, hopeful whisper tapped into his mind. *Tonight.*

Chapter Five

Summer left the meeting by one door, while Drew left by another, and it killed her to see him drive away. It hurt him, too — she could hear his bear's anguished cry the same way she felt his inner pain.

Tonight. She shot the thought out after him. *I'll find you tonight.*

She would have remained standing there for a good hour watching the plume of dust kicked up by his truck rise then slowly fall, but she couldn't. She couldn't afford to show any interest in the bear shifter who'd had the courage to enter this den of wolves.

What had brought Drew to Hope Springs? Was something wrong? She longed to voice the questions racing through her mind.

"Goddamn bear, coming up here like that," Mett grumbled beside her.

She jolted in surprise. Whoops. She'd tuned out of the world for a minute, and that was dangerous. A good thing Mett interpreted her shiver of fear the wrong way.

"Don't you worry, Summ." He slithered an arm over her shoulders and drew her close. "I'll keep you safe."

It was all she could do not to dig an elbow into his ribs to keep him away. Far away.

Drew will keep me safe, she wanted to say. But shit, Drew was driving away, so the only one keeping her safe was herself. She couldn't let Mett catch on to her. Not now

She wrapped her arms around her stomach, trying to create a gap between his body and hers. "Thanks."

"Anything for you, darlin'."

Claws itched under her fingernails as her wolf begged for release.

"Anything for my mate," Mett added, and she froze.

"Mate?"

"Of course, Summ. Don't you feel it, too?"

All she felt was a churning stomach and a yearning for Drew.

"Just think," he said.

She tried really, really hard not to think of the horrors being mated to Mett might entail.

"We can make a new start, and we can continue my dad's work. Carry on the crusade you fought so hard for."

The only thing that made her more nauseous than the idea of being mated to Mett was the idea that she really had assisted the Blue Bloods' sick crusade. She hadn't meant to, yet she had.

A few weeks ago, she would have crumpled in shame at the thought. But she was stronger than that now. Wiser. More determined than ever to set a wrong right.

Tears and regrets wouldn't change the past. All she could do was prevent the same from happening in the future by staying focused. Which meant keeping an eye on the goings-on in this pack and reporting to her friends at the Blue Moon Saloon. And it meant finding Drew to understand what had brought him to Utah. But how on earth was she going to sneak off unnoticed?

Mett tightened his grip on her arm, as if reading her mind.

"I'm just preoccupied about tonight," she bluffed. "Who do you think will win?"

"Doesn't matter," Mett whispered with a sly smile. "I have a plan."

All of a sudden, her whole body went on red alert.

"A plan?"

Mett nodded, looking supremely satisfied with himself. "A plan for both of us."

His eyes shone with a hint of the madness she'd seen in his father at times, and her skin crawled. Still, she forced her body closer to his and ran a finger down his cheek. "What kind of plan?"

He groped her ass and yanked her close enough to feel his growing erection. "Can't tell anyone, baby. But soon, I will."

She wanted to shove herself clear and scrub her skin clean, but she forced herself to play along. "Come on, Mett. You can tell me."

He half whispered, half licked his next words into her ear. "Big secret. Just believe me when I tell you it doesn't matter which of them wins."

Her wolf snarled inside, but she kept the beast under control — barely.

So disgusting. How can you put up with this snake? her wolf cried. He reeked of tobacco and pure, unadulterated hate.

She did it because she had to. She had to find out more. What was Mett plotting? What did he mean?

"You can trust me," she tried, touching his chest.

"Oh, I trust you all right. Don't worry your pretty little head."

That line, she'd heard before. And damn it, she hadn't worried back then. Well, she was worried now. Mett was up to something.

"Now how about you and me—" he started.

"Mett!" one of Gretchen's hulking sons called over. "You and that she-wolf of yours can screw later. Come and help."

Her wolf's snarl grew lower, more dangerous.

"Don't worry," Mett whispered, finally letting her go. "You and me can have fun later."

Sure. Fun. She wanted to slap him, but she forced her reluctant lips into a smile instead. "Can I help?"

What? her wolf screeched.

Better to keep an eye on him, right?

If I'm not sick first, her wolf murmured.

"Sure, Summ. Let's go." He grabbed her hand and towed her along.

We just have to stay in spitting distance, she told her wolf. *See what he's up to.*

Spitting distance? Don't tempt me.

She stuck with him for the rest of the afternoon, enduring more of his lecherous grins and touches. For the most part, though, she kept out of range of his wandering hands, which were mostly full as Mett and his cousins collected wood for a huge bonfire.

"For when the alpha is named," he explained. "Not that it matters much."

She studied him closely, trying to read his mind. What was he up to?

Beside the bonfire, they cleared space for a fighting arena, complete with rough wooden benches and risers.

"Gonna be a hell of a fight," one of his cousins said.

"Yeah. Maybe they'll kill each other," Mett murmured. "Save us the trouble."

Her heart raced, and she wondered if she should tell Thomas. But he was as much of an unknown as Mett.

As the sun dropped closer and closer to the horizon, the crowd grew. Wolf shifters she didn't even recognize showed up, eager to witness the fight. Some of them looked wary, as if they, too, were as concerned about their future as she. They were ordinary shifters, she figured, who wanted to put their pack back on track — an honest track — and move on with their lives. A few younger guns chewed tobacco and chanted their support for one candidate or the other, and those worried her more. They'd follow whatever leader emerged from this mess. But who would that be?

She looked at the building Thomas had disappeared into for the afternoon, then over at the shelter where Dryver and his men waited as the hours ticked past. Finally, her eyes slid over to Mett. He lacked the raw power and brains of the other two, but he seemed so sure of himself. What ace did he have up his sleeve? He didn't talk about his plans to anyone else, but every time he looked at her, he winked.

Right on cue, her stomach rolled.

Once they had set everything up, Mett and his cousins started drinking.

"You want one?" he asked, shoving a warm bottle of beer in her hands.

"No thanks," she managed. "But do you want another?"

He grinned like a man freshly mated to a meek little she-wolf who would be at his beck and call. "Got me a good one, boys," he called to his cousins.

Try me, her wolf murmured inside.

She served drink after drink, doing her best to get Mett as drunk as she could.

"There's more back there, baby," Mett said, waving her toward a building.

Happy for a momentary escape, she entered and looked around. "Oops," she mumbled, entering a bathroom by mistake. She was halfway out the door when she stopped in her tracks.

Bathroom. Cabinet. Drugs.

She darted inside, grabbed the painkillers she found in the cabinet, and headed out to where the liquor was stored. The hard stuff. With shaking hands, she split open capsules and poured the contents into a bottle of vodka, then shook the bottle on her way out.

"Where have you been?" Mett barked, showing his dark side again.

"Getting you the good stuff. Look."

The sun had just slipped over the horizon, and the men had placed torches around the fighting ring. Half a dozen men were already circling each other there, vying to be the first to start the show.

"Half an hour to go," someone murmured.

Mett swiped the bottle from her hand and took a hard swig.

She watched him carefully, edging farther and farther away from the center of action, eyeing everyone around her while trying not to appear suspicious. Fights for an alpha position could take all night, mainly because they were preceded by dozens of lesser fights as men took sides and challenged each other in pairs. Those warm-up fights rarely resulted in death, but they were messy, drawn-out contests between hot-blooded youngsters eager to show off their prowess. More bark than bite for the most part, with contestants fighting in human form before shifting to four feet. One fight would lead to another and another, feeding the crowd's thirst for blood. It would take hours for things to finally escalate to alpha level. She doubted anyone would miss her in the excitement. The trick would be slipping away in the first place.

Mett looked around for her, stumbled, then took another long swig.

Now? her wolf begged, ready to run for the hills.

She checked the scene one more time. Gretchen was on the far side of the arena, paying Summer no mind. Mett sat down on a hay bale, blinking hard. His cousins were drunk, too, even if they hadn't ingested any of the spiked stuff.

Let's go! her wolf urged. *Now!*

She took one last look around then stepped out of sight behind an outlying building. She moved slowly, using one structure after another for cover, leaving the hubbub behind. Finally, she reached the edge of the settlement and jogged up a path, then ran like she was running for her life.

Drew, her wolf hummed. *We get to see Drew!*

Her step faltered before she forced herself onward. What if Drew hadn't been bluffing when he addressed the wolves? What if he had changed his mind about her?

She clenched her jaw and ran on, following a narrow gully that wound northwest. Even if Drew had changed his mind — even if he broke her heart — she had to see him. To share what she'd observed, for starters, and to find out how she might best help whatever mission he had been tasked with.

She stopped, shed her clothes, and hid them behind a rock before shifting to wolf form. And the second she did, instinct took over.

Mate! Must see my mate, her wolf cried as she sniffed the air for any sign of pursuit.

Nothing. No one had seen her go, and no one was following. They were all too busy at the fight, and they'd be busy for hours after with the bonfire and gossip that always followed such landmark events in a pack's history.

And if anyone did follow her... Her fur bristled, and she bared her long teeth. No one was stopping her tonight.

She splashed across a creek and waded a long way upstream, exiting and reentering the water several times to make sure she couldn't be tracked. Then she flicked her trail, jogged up a hill, and sniffed.

She couldn't scent Drew from here — not directly. But every muscle in her body sensed a pull coming from the east, so she ran that way full tilt.

Mate, her wolf huffed as she ran. He was out there. He was waiting for her.

She ran faster and faster, willing him to hear her call. *Wait for me, my mate.*

Chapter Six

Drew shifted from foot to foot and peered through the darkness. Where was she?

He kicked the ground for the tenth time and paced toward the road, then back up the trail. He'd driven miles from Hope Springs to a tiny state park that seemed as good a place as any for a clandestine meeting. But would Summer even show?

He scratched his ear and told himself not to doubt her. But hell, he had done a pretty good job keeping a poker face at the wolf pack meeting, not to mention making vague enough comments about mixing shifter species that she might have bought into his deceit. But surely Summer would know he was firmly on his cousin's side. She wouldn't turn her back on him, would she?

He checked the perimeter again and went back to pacing. The only sound was the crunch of his boots over the dusting of snow on the ground. He sniffed the air to make sure there was no one else around. And why would there be, way up this back road to a remote corner of the park? He'd let himself through a few poorly locked gates on the way in, parked a good mile away, hopped a fence, and hid his tracks carefully. No way was anyone going to interrupt them tonight.

Trust me, the voice in his mind whispered. *You are safe here.*

Well, he'd be the judge of that. He triple-checked everything until his bear was satisfied.

Safe. His bear nodded. *But where is she?*

He'd felt the pull to this place. Did Summer, too? There was a hum coming from the ground — almost from the center of the earth. As if Mother Nature had guided him to this special place, eager to facilitate a secret rendezvous.

He checked his watch and then the area yet again. The clearing he stood in held a couple of picnic tables with grills, and none of the ashes were new. The area was officially closed anyway, and most importantly, there was no hint of shifters here.

No, he didn't have to worry. He was alone.

Don't want alone, his bear sighed sadly. *Want my mate.*

That was the problem. There was no hint of Summer, either.

Patience, he barked at his bear, complete hypocrite that he was.

Finally, the bushes at the far side of the clearing rustled, and he spun.

"Summer."

Her name was about all he could manage when she stepped out of the shadows. It was her. It had to be her. But Jesus, he'd never seen her in wolf form before. And that wolf — Summer — took his breath away.

She was just as beautiful as he expected. Her hair was just as fair as he was used to seeing, which made her lighter than any wolf he'd ever seen. Her eyes were that same chocolate brown, but they were even more intense than usual, and all the more striking with the slightly darker stripe of fur that marked the line of her brow. Her nose was black and shiny, and her nostrils flared, taking in his scent. She held her body exactly as she held her human form: tall and a little stiff, like someone who felt fear but refused to bow to it.

Fear. He was determined to erase that from her life. Someday. Somehow. Yes, it was risky, meeting like this. But not meeting was riskier, because he couldn't keep his passion for her bottled up any more. This seemed like the only way — getting the need out of his system before sneaking back to the Blue Blood stronghold and caging away his desire again.

His bear rumbled, encouraging her to sniff all she wanted. *You're mine, and I'm yours.* Did she feel it, too?

"Summer," he said, letting his voice break the silence of the forest.

He held his breath, admiring every detail of the wolf. Imprinting them all onto his memory. Her long legs, the glint of starlight in her eyes. The hopeful expression on her face.

"Summer," he whispered, coaxing her forward.

She licked her wolf lips and flicked her tail back and forth. Slowly, she took a step, and the moonlight shimmered over her coat. Another step, and Drew still hadn't dared to exhale. He hadn't even dared to think. He just stood there, lost in her spell.

She was all the way across the clearing, and that seemed much, much too far. But thankfully, she was coming closer, one cautious step at a time. She seemed to be getting taller, too, and at first, he thought it was a trick of the light — that the shimmer around her was her wolf's body heat wavering in the cold air. Then he realized she was shifting, and he gaped. Shifters didn't just change forms around anyone. Only around packmates and their most trusted friends.

"Summer," he whispered in a voice thick with gratitude and wonder.

As she reared up on her hind legs, her human features emerged. She flexed her paws as they elongated into fingers and hands. Her beautiful wolf pelt receded, leaving her skin bare, and she wrapped her arms around herself. Against the cold or because of his stare? Both?

He gulped, unable to drag his eyes away from the sleek lines and creamy skin of Summer, the woman. So stunning, she looked like Venus rising from the ocean. So radiant, she flipped around his sense of seasons and hours. Instead of the cold of winter, he felt the warmth of July, and the space around her practically glowed, as if that was the sun shining down into that clearing instead of the nearly full moon.

Her skin was pale and smooth, her legs long and slender, her nipples tight in the cold. They pointed up slightly, peeking between her fingers, and his lips moved involuntarily. He longed for a taste. He longed to touch the swell of her breasts and the endlessly long legs that stretched to the graceful curve of her hips.

His bear chuffed inside. *Mine. Mate.*

Thank goodness for whatever instinct made him whip off his jacket and wrap it around her shoulders. Maybe she wouldn't take him for a total caveman.

The thing was, he didn't just place the jacket over her shoulders. He wrapped his arms around her, too, and she squeezed in immediately. So tightly, he could feel the push of her nipples against his shirt. So close, he could feel the warmth of her belly and chest. So intimately, his bear got all kinds of bad ideas.

"Hi," she murmured.

When he'd spoken, his voice seemed to invade the peaceful space, but Summer's seemed part of it, like the whisper of one branch over another or the soft flutter of a bird's wings. But there was a sad note to it, too, and that gutted him. There was so much he wanted to say, but none of it came out.

Summer, put the past behind you. Step into the future with me.

Summer, you're the most amazing person I've ever met. Don't you know that?

Summer, I dream about us sharing a life together. Do you dream it, too?

"Hi," was all he could get out. "You found me."

A shy smile spread across her face, warming him. "I found you."

He wanted to ask how, hoping it was her heart and not her nose that had led her here. But they didn't have all night, and he really ought to get down to business, right?

We have a couple of hours, at least, his bear growled. *Plenty of time.*

"You found me," he echoed like a complete dunce, and her smile grew.

Every instinct told him to step even closer and share his body heat with her. But damn it — habit made him take half a step back. Somehow, that always happened. That back-and-forth. It was as if his inner bear couldn't get close enough to Summer and wanted to erase the distance between them, while his human side knew he had to give her space. She was her own person, not his, and he couldn't presume she wanted him as badly as he wanted her.

But damn, did he hope she did.

"You always do that," she murmured, pulling him closer.

"Do what?"

"Step close, then step away." She pulled again, inviting him into her space. So close, she had to tip back her head to look at him. Or more precisely, to look at his lips.

"You're cold," he murmured.

She shook her head and gave him a naughty grin. "I'm hot."

He groaned inside. How the hell was a bear supposed to control himself in a situation like this?

"No need for control," she whispered, tickling his ear with her lips. "Not tonight."

He did a double take. Could she read his mind now? Or had the look on his face given him away?

No need for control, his bear echoed as she unbuttoned his shirt.

"I need this so bad," she whispered. Her breath hung before her, a tiny cloud of condensation in the crisp night air.

See? his bear chuffed. *She wants us. Needs us.*

He pulled her closer, wrapping her in his warmth. He didn't dare ask what *this* was, though he could see it in her eyes. He could feel it in the pull of her body on his.

She slid a hand up his chest, and it caught in the fabric of his shirt. A shirt he was ready to tear the rest of the way off — anything to be skin to skin with her.

"Drew," she whispered. "I need you so much."

Her eyes were aflame, and her breath hitched just like his did. His cock hardened in his jeans, pushing against the denim.

Summer, he nearly said. *I need you, too.*

He wanted so much. Her body. Her love. Her company, day in and day out. He wanted a future with her. He wanted her as his mate.

But if that didn't make him a greedy prick, what did?

So he backtracked and focused on her. "Tell me what you need. Tell me what you want."

"You," she said, letting her hand stray downward again. She rested it on his abdomen, a good six inches higher than he would have liked. "I want us." Then a cloud passed over her eyes. "But I'm scared, too."

"Of what?"

"Remember who I am, Drew."

Well, that was easy. "You're the most amazing person I know. The person I want."

She stared at him then shook her head. "Isn't it wrong for me to want you after what I did?"

"You did what you were forced to do. And wrong?" He took her by the shoulders. "You didn't do anything. Hate is wrong. Love. . . Love is right."

"Love?"

He nodded firmly. "God, Summer. From the second I met you, I wanted you. I still want you. For forever, I mean."

She bit her lip. "I knew it before I even saw you. Even before you stepped in the door, I knew."

"So why fight it? Don't you feel it, too?"

"I feel it," she murmured, but she still looked so sad. As if she was determined to deny herself happiness for the rest of her life.

No way, his bear growled. *Not letting her do that.*

Without thinking, he stepped closer, barely leaving an inch of empty space between their chests.

"You feel this, right?" he asked in a husky voice. *This* was the heat that built between them, the crackle and lick of invisible flames.

Her eyes fluttered, telling him she did. And how could she miss it? He could feel the threads of destiny wrap around them both like the strands of a cocoon. He could hear the earthy voice of fate chanting, *mate, mate, mate.*

He wrapped his arms around her before she could revisit her past, then dropped his chin until he was within kissing distance of her rosy lips.

"You must feel this," he said, sweeping his hand through the space between them. "This energy. This need. The call."

"The call..."

"The call of my mate."

There. He'd finally said it. She might slap him or call him crazy or run away, but at least he'd said it.

"Mate?" Her lips trembled.

"Mate," he said.

His bear gave him a high five.

Summer took a deep breath and nodded. "I feel it. I want it, too."

The words just about made him explode. She wanted him, too!

Every star in the sky seemed to cheer him on. *So kiss her! Kiss her! Come on!*

He leaned in slowly enough for her to pull away, but she didn't.

"I want it, too," she echoed quietly. "So much."

Enough of a green light for you? his bear demanded.

The dam in him broke, and a tingle of anticipation zipped through his chest.

He figured he'd better go for the world's softest kiss, but they ended up coming together with a bang, because she reached forward at exactly the same time as him. And for one shaky second, their lips searched awkwardly for the perfect fit. But the moment they did...

Summer moaned and shifted closer. Her breasts squeezed against his chest, her hips swung forward, teasing his cock. Her hands ran up and down his arms. She opened her mouth the same moment he did, letting him taste deeply.

He wrapped his arms around her and let them travel slowly down. And down and down to the perfect curve of her ass. Summer moaned, and he nearly did, too.

Make her do that again, his bear demanded. *I need to hear her want us. Do it again.*

He reached a little farther down, spreading his fingers wide, and then shuffled one leg forward to spread hers apart.

Summer made a needy, desperate sound, and he did, too. He couldn't see. He couldn't think. All he could do was inhale her heady scent. God, the taste of her — like all the flavors of summer, wrapped into one. Honey. Strawberries. Rose hip tea, warmed by the sun. Like freedom, because that had a taste, too, even if it was harder to pin down.

"Drew," she murmured, sliding her arms behind his neck. Not just his shoulders but his neck, demanding he kiss her harder. Deeper.

He smothered her in a kiss that had been waiting days — weeks, even — to be released. So it wasn't gentle and it wasn't soft, but neither was hers. When she reached under his shirt to touch his skin, his blood rushed, and he consumed her in another kiss. Really *consumed* her like he could never get enough. He backed her right up to the edge of a picnic table while she stripped him out of his shirt. Even then, he kept going, just barely hanging on to his self-control.

"Drew," she whispered again and again.

He spread his shirt on the picnic table behind her and kept right on kissing and touching and leaning until she was flat on her back. He pulled away just long enough to check that she was all in.

"I'm all in, bear," she murmured, pulling him closer.

Damn. Had she read his mind?

More, his bear demanded. *Want more!*

"Help me with these," she whispered, yanking at his jeans.

He kicked off his boots and jeans and cast them aside, and when his boxers followed, his cock stood straight up.

Take her! his bear screamed. *Need my mate!*

"Drew." Summer curled into a half sit-up. Her eyes fluttered to his erection, and when she met his gaze again, her face was flushed, her lips parted.

I want that, the glow in her eyes said. *I want you inside.*

And man, he'd never felt such a rush in his life.

"You sure you want this?" he managed.

She laughed and settled down on her back, laying herself out like a feast. "Do I look sure?"

She lifted both legs until her heels rested on the edge of the table. She bent her knees, opening her core, inviting him in.

Yeah, she looked sure, all right.

He bent over her body. One more kiss with some measure of control, and then he'd give in to his animal side. One kiss to tell her this was more than just one body craving another.

This was about him and her. About the future. About love.

His lips covered hers, and she rose under him, reaching for his cock. She stroked it gently, the way his tongue stroked over her lips. But then her grip grew harder, the way his movements did.

More, his bear agreed.

He plundered her mouth and tugged her body closer to the table's edge. Then he practically kissed her through the table until her moans filled his ears. She clutched him the whole time, telling him to keep going, not to hold back.

And there was no holding back now, anyway. Not with his bear firmly in control. He nibbled his way down her neck and chest until he was gorging on her right breast, scooping the flesh closer, flicking his tongue over her tight little nipple. It hardened immediately and stood erect in his mouth as he laved his tongue over it again and again.

"Drew," she moaned, arching into his touch.

His heart pounded in his chest. His brain sent a thousand mixed messages, ordering him to touch her in a thousand different ways at once. More of her soft breasts. More of the flat expanse of her abdomen. He found himself licking her belly button without even remembering how he got there. He bobbed back up, suckling from her breast, then dipped down, spreading her legs with his hands.

"Drew," she cried, guiding his head lower.

He spread her with his thumbs. Rested his head against her inner thigh and let his chin scrub a path all the way to her core, where he inhaled her scent, then flicked his tongue.

She tasted like honey. Like berries, ripe for the picking. Like home. He got drunk on that taste and sucked it up —

desperately, like a bear feasting at the onset of fall, because who knew what the future would hold.

Summer jolted against him, and her hands fluttered over his shoulders, begging him to go on.

"Yes. Please, yes," she murmured again and again.

So he licked. Sucked. Practically drank — and drank and drank, like a goddamn castaway in the desert. Like a knight with the Holy Grail. He consumed her like no man had ever consumed a woman before.

He wasn't even aware of his own movements, only her responses. The buck of her hips. The pressure of her hands. The quiver of her skin. When he drove his fingers deep, she sucked in a shaky breath. And when his lips zeroed in on the nub of her clit, she cried out desperately. Her whole body writhed and danced as he gulped and feasted until he was drunk and gorged. Drunk on his pleasure and on hers.

My mate likes this. Loves this, his bear chuckled inside.

He could tell from the play of her fingers over his back, the tight grip of her thighs around his head. She was arched so far back, he could scoop both hands around her ass and keep her close, like a greedy man holding a platter up to his mouth.

"Please," she begged. "I'm so close."

Any other woman would have been limp and exhausted by then, but Summer hung on and on, denying herself release as if she could sense how much more he wanted to learn about her.

He teased her, traveling from her sweet core to her pink, peaked nipples and back again until her belly was red with scrub marks from his beard. He didn't just want to make her feel good. He wanted to launch her straight off the earth. So he explored, discovering what moved her, what shook her, and what brought her to the edge of joyous tears. He memorized all the combinations, piece by delicious piece, until he was finally ready to put it all together and let her fly.

"Drew," she gasped, and her voice shot higher.

Yeah, she was close, all right.

He slipped two fingers deep inside her and curled them against a spot that made her leap halfway out of her skin, then massaged her clit with his tongue. Harder, faster — the way her body demanded. And when he caught the nub of it between his lips—

"Drew," she moaned, exploding beneath him.

He hung on, lapping up her juices, gripping her body, listening to the sounds she made. Just when he thought she might waft back down from her high, he pushed in again with his fingers and tongue to wring a second orgasm out of her, right on the heels of the first. And when she came out of that one, panting and limp and murmuring incoherently, he laid his head on her belly and held her tight.

My woman, his bear growled, ridiculously pleased with himself. *My mate.*

His highly satisfied mate. He could hear it in her dreamy sigh, feel it in her needy touch. Yes, his cock was aching for its own release, but that could wait. The world could wait, damn it. He wrapped his arms around her, closed his eyes, and breathed her in.

"Beautiful," he murmured.

"Beautiful," she echoed in a dreamy, faraway voice.

He smiled into her stomach, drew a heart with a finger, and tried not to get carried away with thoughts of the future. This was just one night. One little night.

A night he would draw out forever if he could.

Chapter Seven

"Drew." Summer slid her tongue over her lips, savoring the taste of him. She'd been flying through the stratosphere, barely able to speak after the high he'd licked her into. She paused for a quick check, just in case. Were her lips working again? Could she produce more than a moan or a cry?

"Drew," she whispered.

Lips, check. Fingers?

They flexed and traced a hard line of muscle on his arm.

Girl parts?

Her body gave a slow, sultry thumbs-up.

She figured she was ready to croak something other than his name. But what?

Drew's fingers moved across her skin, sending little ripples through her overwhelmed nerves. One by one, her synapses woke up, going from la-la land to...to...

Shit, to all-out desire.

She lay perfectly still as a second heat wave roared through her body. Was it even possible to want more after an orgasm like that?

Her wolf stirred inside and flicked its tail from side to side.

Apparently so.

Maybe she'd blame it all on the three-quarters-full moon, shining on her like a spotlight from above. Stars crowded around, winking like so many Peeping Toms. The clearing was surrounded by pines, their boughs drooping with snow — a reminder that, technically, she ought to feel cold. But Drew lay over her like a lead blanket, keeping her warm. The jut of his cock against her thigh told her he was giving her a chance to recover before seeking his own pleasure. Pleasure she didn't want to deny him a minute longer.

She shifted under him and let a foot snake up his leg.

"Summer…"

Her stomach heated under his muffled breath, and her whole body prickled with the realization of how hungry she suddenly felt. Starving. Ravenous. Desperate for him to fill her over and over again.

"At the risk of sounding bossy…" she ventured.

He picked his head up and looked at her with eyes that blazed.

"I want you inside me. Now. Please."

And she didn't mean with his fingers or tongue — as unbelievably satisfying as that had been. She wanted it all. She needed to be filled. Stretched. She needed to feel the full force of him pounding into her, again and again. Every thick, hot inch of him.

She shook her head at herself. Since when did she have such a dirty mind?

Pretty simple, her wolf shot back. *Since we met our mate.*

She'd been with a few men in her time — hell, every she-wolf had her needs — but she'd never, ever been as hungry, as screw-or-die desperate as she was right now. Her wolf was yowling inside, begging for more.

"Need you to fill me, my mate," she whispered.

A rumble built in his chest, and heat flared between her legs.

"Drew," she begged, guiding him closer with her legs and hands. Trembling with anticipation as his body lined up with hers. "Come to me, bear."

The grumble grew deeper, and his cock nudged against her folds. She was wet enough for him to glide right in, but damn it, he was doing that slow-and-careful thing again. Like the routine he'd developed when entering the café. That hesitation on the threshold, that stepping up then stepping back.

"Don't tell me you're turning into a gentleman now," she groaned.

He shook his head vehemently. "Not a chance. Just admiring."

"Admiring what?"

She'd never, ever seen Drew look greedy before now, and damn did it turn her on.

"You," he whispered, smoothing her hair back from her face.

His gaze traveled down her body, heating her every inch of the way. His lips cracked open when he focused on her breasts, as if he hadn't already spent long, luscious minutes worshiping them, and her nipples peaked all over again.

"Admiring you," he whispered.

She lifted her hips off the table and pushed against him, demanding more. "I need you inside me. I need you so much."

His expression went from wondrous to wicked as he wrapped his huge hands around her hips, took a deep breath—

She took a deep breath, too.

—and pushed into her with one smooth thrust.

"Yes," she cried at the sweet burn inside. The stretch, the perfect balance of pleasure and pain. "Drew."

He pulled back an inch then slid in two. Back one, in two, moving in gradual steps that echoed his manner of approaching her in the café. Carefully. Slowly, as if savoring the sensation.

He set into a steady rhythm, and the need to speed into another high receded. Maybe she should savor, too. She'd been in such a rush, but suddenly, all she wanted was to rock with him for another hour or two. She adjusted the angle of her heels against his ass, and he followed her cue, pulling her whole body closer while thrusting deeper still.

Although her eyes were closed, soft white light filled her vision. Heaven. She was on her way to heaven.

Drew leaned over her body, and his heavy breaths whooshed past her ears. She could picture the puffs of condensation in the cold winter air, though all she felt was heat. Every inch of her, on fire for him.

"Drew," she murmured. "Deeper."

He was already deeper than she'd ever had a man before, and it burned, but still, she needed more. He needed more, too. She spread her knees wider, and he lifted them over his shoulders, finding the perfect angle.

"Oh, yes." It was all she could do not to scream the words over and over now that Drew had picked up speed.

Deeper. Harder, her wolf begged. *Want every inch of my mate.*

The next time he pumped, she clenched down with her inner muscles, slowing his penetration to a delicious crawl.

He groaned against her neck, and she cracked into a grin.

"Like that?" she teased.

"Love that," he said in a rough, gritty voice.

"So do it again."

He pushed up on his elbows. *Anything you desire.*

She stared. Was that his bear she'd heard?

Drew's eyes glowed with sheer animal power. A look she'd never seen on her quiet, reserved bear before. A look she wouldn't mind unleashing a little more often.

Like, for a lifetime, her wolf murmured.

She spread her hands across the thick muscles of his ass and nodded.

"Oh!" she cried when he hammered to a spot he hadn't touched before.

"Okay?" he asked through his next groan.

Was he kidding? "Okay is not the word."

He liked that. She could tell from the sparks in his eyes, the upward curl at the corners of his mouth. And damn, did she love this version of her bear. Well, she loved both versions, but this side of him was wilder. Naughtier. More demanding. She'd have to get him hot and naked more often.

"Watch what you wish for," he teased, reading her mind.

"Watch. I like the sound of that." She tucked her chin and fixed her eyes on the point of their connection. It felt deliciously dirty, watching him slide in and out of her.

Maybe they were both discovering their wild sides. A dozen ambitious positions flashed through her mind. Like Drew lifting her against a wall while pounding into her again and again. Or of her dropping to her knees and taking him in her mouth. Or running through the woods in the best kind of chase. Or...or...

Her mind went blank then, and she realized the only thing she wanted was exactly this way, right now.

We'll save the other ideas for later. Her wolf grinned.

Drew withdrew and waited, poised at her entrance. She shivered, watching the thick mass of him appear, inch by throbbing inch. His cock glistened, and his hands tightened on her hips.

God, he was a work of art. And Jesus, was he big.

Big, but a perfect fit, her wolf added.

"Drew—" she started just as he thrust forward, making her vision blur. She tightened her muscles, milking him every inch of the way.

"So good," he said, pushing her to her limits.

She gasped and held on tight. It was beyond good. It was lightning, fire, and thunder to her soul.

"Again. Please. Please do that again."

He pulled back, then hammered back in, clenching his teeth.

"Don't stop. Please don't stop," she begged, clutching his shoulders, digging in with her heels.

He pulled out, and his eyes flashed with a look that said, *I never want to stop.*

"More," she gulped, clamping her legs around him. "More."

"More," he replied in a hoarse voice, giving it to her. His thrusts grew faster and harder. Jerkier, too, as he slowly lost control. She tucked her chin and watched him pound into her. Noises escaped her — desperate little mewing sounds like a greedy kitten.

Drew rocked faster and faster, and she would have jolted over the picnic table each time if he hadn't held her so close. He reached around to pull her right leg higher, changing the angle, and she cried out as he bottomed out in a whole new spot.

He might have cried out, too. She couldn't tell any more, because her ears were filled with that roaring sound again, her whole body about to melt down.

"More," she begged, although she was sure she'd explode any second.

His eyes flickered with a deep-seated hunger, and sweat broke out on his brow.

"Drew," she murmured, thrusting forward as he powered in, making it more of a slam than a slide.

Her head fell back as every muscle in her body coiled for the release building inside her. Did he feel the pressure, too? Did he see the blinding light that shone into every corner of her body, making her feel incredibly alive?

"Summer," he groaned, thrusting one more time.

She moaned as her whole body shuddered with unbearable pleasure. Drew shuddered, too, emptying inside her. His heat spread through her as her body sang and danced and raved.

"Yes," she moaned, drawing out the high, memorizing the moment. The heat of his body inside hers. The tight grip of his hands on her waist. The stiffness of his body as he gloried in his own release.

Yes, her wolf cried, and her fangs pressed on the inside of her gums, begging to be unleashed. She found herself eyeing his neck, planning where to bite. A mating bite. A bond that would make him hers forever.

Drew was eyeing her neck, too, and she saw his bear wrestling for control.

Yes, she swore she could hear the beast murmur. *A mating bite. Let me make you mine.*

His nostrils flared, and she almost tipped her head back in invitation. *Make me yours, Drew. Forever.*

But an owl hooted, and a tiny dusting of snow sprinkled down from one of the boughs overhead. A reminder of the stark reality around them.

"We can't," he croaked, coming to his senses, too. "Not yet."

The *yet* was the only part of the sentence she liked. But he was right. They were already risking too much by meeting like this.

She cupped his cheeks and kissed him long and hard.

"Not yet," she conceded. "But someday..."

He nodded and cuddled her closer. "Someday soon."

She looked up at the sky and sighed. The stars seemed brighter, the air crisper, the night darker than before. Was it her, feeling more alive than before, or had the universe changed, too?

"Come on," Drew said, untangling his limbs from hers.

"Wait," she protested. She loved the weight of his body over hers. She loved the closeness, the way his chest rose and fell beside hers.

"I promise you this will be worth it," he said, pulling her to her feet.

She shivered, feeling the cold for the first time since she'd shifted from her wolf form. "Where are we going?"

"You'll see." He kept his hand tight around hers as he led her down the path.

The night was crystal clear, but the woods ahead of them were swirling with mist, and she hesitated. What was hiding back there, out of sight?

"Trust me," he murmured.

She hung back for a split second, then gave in. Of course, she could trust her mate.

"You don't think I brought you here for the picnic tables, did you?" He grinned.

Well, that piqued her curiosity. "I liked the picnic table. Loved it, in fact."

He squeezed her hand. "Me, too. But this is even better. I promise."

A few steps more, and she could barely see through the witch's broth of condensation. She held his hand tighter than ever.

"Um, Drew..."

"Here." He motioned to a wooden frame that lay flat, squaring off a patch of earth.

She looked closer. Wait, that wasn't earth. It was water, and it was steaming.

"Hot springs," Drew whispered. His voice carried on the mist.

The tension in her shoulders disappeared, and she laughed out loud. "Hot springs?" Maybe her bear was more adventurous than she thought.

"Come on," he said.

She slid into the steamy water, oohing and ahhing at the warmth.

"Not bad, huh?" he asked.

"Not bad," she agreed, sliding closer.

Drew sat on the submerged bench built into the pool, and she straddled his lap.

"Not bad," she murmured. His cock twitched against her core, and she ground against him, suddenly craving more.

"Not bad," he whispered, holding her hips.

A second later, they were connected again, both of them rocking and sweating and murmuring in pleasure. Drew lapped at her nipples, flipping every switch in her on. She pumped over him, ever faster and harder, and when he tipped his head all the way back, she did the same.

"Yes," she murmured as his thickness filled her. Filled her like no man ever had before.

"Yes," he murmured, letting her take the lead for another glorious minute. Then he stood up with a mighty splash and drew her out of the water.

"I get the top," he growled, laying her out along the wooden frame.

She wrapped her arms and legs around him, rising to meet his body.

"Summer," he murmured as he slid in.

He said her name again and again, even as he pounded her into another incredible high.

"Summer," he breathed afterward, holding her close.

"Mate," she whispered, feeling the full meaning of the word for the very first time.

Yes, he was a bear. Yes, they were playing with fire, allowing things to go this far.

And no, she'd never regret it. No matter what lay ahead.

Chapter Eight

"See you soon," she whispered an hour later when they dragged themselves out of bliss and back into reality.

If only she didn't have to leave the hot springs where they'd been wrapped around each other like a couple of cubs in a cozy den.

We don't have to, her wolf had whispered. *We can stay and stay and stay.*

No, she couldn't. She had to get back to Hope Springs and see what had come of the fight. She had to find Mett and figure out what he was planning.

Drew's eyes shimmered with a mix of pure sorrow and staunch duty. "I don't want to go, either. But we have to."

They drew apart slowly and formed a rough plan which started with scrubbing themselves fiercely in the water. There was no way they could carry the slightest whiff of each other's scent back to the wolf pack.

He grimaced. "I can stop in a bar on the way back and make sure I smell like alcohol and smoke."

She nodded. "I'll roll in every skunkbush I can find."

Don't leave him! her wolf howled.

She had to. They were close to finishing their mission. Close to discovering what the future course of Hope Springs was. She couldn't let herself quit now. Not even for her mate.

"See you soon," he whispered.

They both stood there for a long time, looking at each other. Finally, Summer shifted into wolf form and forced herself to go with a firm shake of her coat.

She hadn't slept a wink, but fear and curiosity gripped her, and once she was out of sight of Drew, she ran like a woman possessed. Had anyone at Hope Springs noticed her absence? What had happened with the fight? What would happen next?

Drew had told her about the anonymous appeal for help they'd received at the saloon. Was there really someone committed to finishing off the Blue Blood movement once and for all? If so, who? Thomas? One of the elders? Someone else who'd been biding their time so far? Or was it a ruse?

But first things first. She didn't even know which of the contenders won the fight for alpha position. And the longer she thought about it, the faster she moved, anxious to find out. She ran long and hard, not letting her pace flag until she crested the last rise and stopped at the view. The sun was just peeking over the horizon, lighting the lower sky with a pinkish-yellow glow. Open country stretched as far as the eye could see, and a single set of headlights marked the state highway at this lonely hour. The earth sloped upward from south to north, and ribbons of color stood out in the rocky bluffs, showing off eons of nature at work. It was beautiful. Breathtakingly beautiful.

But when she focused on the dusty settlement of Hope Springs, her face set into hard lines. The place looked so quiet, so serene, but she knew it was anything but. She sniffed and caught the scent of wolf musk, even from half a mile away. No surprise there, given the way fights pumped up every male's testosterone — not just the men fighting but those spectating, too. The arena was mostly deserted, though two torches still flickered faintly, and the last embers of a bonfire glowed beside it, still crackling with news of the new alpha to the world.

Which alpha? she wanted to scream. Who won? Logic told her it would be Thomas, but veterans like Dryver were impossible to dismiss. She shook herself again, jogged down the slope, turned a corner—

And ran right into Mett.

She recoiled immediately, and he looked at her through narrow-lidded eyes.

"I was looking for you everywhere," he barked.

Yeah, well, I was avoiding you like the plague, she wanted to say.

"I really needed a run," she explained, sticking to a version of the truth. "But I got lost."

As if I'd ever get lost, her wolf sniffed.

She shushed it before the lie showed and let her gaze drop away from Mett's bloodshot, hungover eyes. Let him think she was sorry or embarrassed or meek. Let him think anything it took to pull off her mission.

"You missed the fight." Gretchen strode up, wearing a deep frown of disapproval.

"I've seen enough fighting," she replied, forcing herself not to glare at the older woman.

"And you nearly missed the meeting." Mett grabbed her arm so hard, his fingernails bit into her skin.

She held back a yelp — and the punch she would have loved to plant on his chin.

"Meeting?" She looked around.

So that's why the place seemed so quiet. Almost everyone was in the barn, and the last stragglers were hurrying in that direction.

"You can sit with us," Gretchen said. An order, not an invitation.

Summer was still considering how to extract herself from those two when a deep voice sounded at her side.

"Kiss for the winner?"

She spun and found Thomas there. So he had won. He looked weary yet triumphant, and his eyes sparkled. And whoa – not just from the win. His eyes sparkled to see her.

Shit, shit, shit.

"Um...uh..." she sputtered. How was she going to get out of all this? Half the women in the pack would have wished themselves into her position at that moment, but Summer just felt sick. She didn't want Thomas any more than she wanted Mett. She wanted Drew. Only Drew. Forever.

But Thomas had already nudged Mett to the side — seething, red-faced Mett — and leaned so close, she had no choice but to give him a peck on the cheek. He smelled of shaving cream and leather polish, like a cowboy who'd just spiffed himself up. Not too bad, really, but nothing like Drew.

For the first second, Thomas was a warm, gentle presence at her side, but a moment later, he went stiff. Shit – had he picked up on Drew's scent? Had she blown her cover?

"Um, what's going on?" She pulled away quickly and motioned to the people hurrying toward the barn.

"I've called a meeting," Thomas said. His eyes narrowed on her, and his nostrils flared.

She trembled inside. She'd been sure to brush off every trace of Drew's scent, but a girl couldn't swim in ecstasy all night and completely hide what she'd been up to. Did she still have that telltale glow, that sleepy scent of bliss?

She tried changing the subject. "A meeting? With who?"

"I've put out a call to every pack in the Four Corners and Nevada," Thomas said, looking every bit the powerful alpha.

"Don't see why we need outsiders meddling in our business," Gretchen grumbled.

Thomas ignored her completely, hooked his arm through Summer's, and strode toward the barn. She followed, trying to stifle her panic. The last thing she needed was an unknown alpha making a claim on her. Thomas had already grabbed control of the pack — who knew what he'd claim next?

Out of the corner of her eye, Summer saw a stiff, heavily bruised Dryver being helped into his truck by his men.

"You should have killed him," Gretchen grumbled. The woman was like a leech at her side, and judging by the expression on Thomas' face, he felt the same.

"No need to kill a good man," he said.

Summer wondered what his definition of a good man was. Good as long as he didn't mix with different species of shifters? Emmett Whyte had seemed fairly normal as long as he was around wolf-only company. So who knew what Thomas meant?

She walked along, wearing a neutral expression and keeping her eyes on the ground. Thomas only released her when they reached the barn door, and the second they stepped through, she hustled to one side. It took her a minute to adjust to the dim interior after the bright light of daybreak, but her nose was immediately filled with the scents of dozens of shifters. Some familiar, others unknown.

"Wow, they're all here," someone nearby murmured.

She blinked, looking around. Who was they?

"Connor Davis of Las Alamitos pack," a man murmured and pointed out the alpha. "Jack Hunter of Indian Ridge. Roric of Westend Pack," the man went on, naming a handful of others.

"Wow. Did they drive through the night?" Summer couldn't help whispering.

"Where have you been, girl?" another person scolded.

Been screwing my mate all night, her wolf purred inside.

"Word is that Thomas put the call out yesterday, before the fight. Cocky son of a bitch."

She looked at Thomas, who was talking with one of the elders. Cocky wasn't the word. Confident, yes, but cautious too. A careful planner who left little to chance. If only he didn't hold his cards so close to his chest.

"Wouldn't you know it," the man continued. "There's that bear, back here again."

Her head snapped up, and she drew in a sharp breath when Drew entered through a door on the opposite side. The crowd murmured, and several wolf shifters skittered out of range of his claws, just in case.

Mate! her wolf cried. *Mate!*

Her eyes locked with his, and for the space of a heartbeat, she was transported back to the magic of the previous night. That feeling of safety, of undying love. His perfect lips quirked, and she smiled, remembering his whispers and his sweet caress.

Then – shit – she wiped the smile off her face and dragged her gaze away. Drew did, too. It had only been a split-second indiscretion, but if anyone noticed...

She looked around, but everyone's eyes seemed to be on Thomas and the elders at the front. Whew. She exhaled—

Then froze when she spotted Thomas, staring at her. His eyes slid over to Drew, then back to her.

Her heart pounded. Her feet felt glued to the ground. Her mind calculated the distance to the door. Thomas knew. He'd figured out her connection to Drew. And damn, did he look angry.

She expected him to shout and sound the alarm, but he just stared at her. And stared and stared with eyes that felt close to boring through her soul.

She kept waiting for her cover to be blown, but Thomas didn't say anything.

Yet.

He could ruin everything. He could turn the crowd on her and Drew in an instant, and even her mighty bear wouldn't stand a chance against dozens of outraged wolves. Drew would be torn apart, and she... Shit. She'd be lucky to be torn apart. If she was unlucky, she'd be spared and forced to mate with Thomas. She'd seen the interest in his eyes, and she'd heard the stories of powerful alphas who took whatever and whomever they wanted.

She was about to turn and flee when his expression went from thunderous to...sad?

Do you think so little of me? She couldn't hear his thoughts in her mind, but she could read them all over his face.

She didn't know what to think. All she wanted was Drew. And peace. Peace in her soul, peace for the shifter world.

"This meeting is called to order," one of the elders cried out.

Thomas turned away from her and raised his hands, signaling for the crowd to listen. He waited until the room was so quiet, she could hear the breath of the man beside her.

She could feel the weight of Drew's gaze upon her, too, and thank goodness for that. It was the only thing keeping her from racing out the door. Was Thomas really not going to challenge the love of two shifters of different species?

Thomas spoke in a voice that was all power, all determination. "As new alpha of Hope Springs pack, I have called in the major packs of the Southwest."

No wonder there were so many newcomers in the room. Thomas had called them in as witnesses not just to the start of his reign, but for some big announcement. The room tingled with anticipation as a dozen grizzled alphas looked on.

"This pack has made a name for itself—"

Thomas paused when a man tiptoed up to him and whispered in his ear. A second later, the barn door burst open, and everyone's heads snapped up.

"Holy shit," someone whispered.

"Fuck."

"Man, oh man."

Even Summer stared.

"The wolves of Twin Moon pack," someone cried.

Five imposing shifters crowded through the door. Big. Menacing. Unamused.

Ty Hawthorne, the tall alpha of Twin Moon pack, glared the room into silence. Beside him was an equally imposing man — Zack, the wolf-coyote tracker. Summer had met him a few times at the saloon. They were flanked by their mates, two women who could have stepped straight from a history book about Amazon warriors, they looked so fierce. One even carried a bow.

"Mistress of the Hunt..." someone murmured in a voice filled with awe.

Summer had met all of them, but dang. In the saloon, they'd been nice, friendly folk. Now, they were all raw, looming power and barely bridled rage.

Behind the four wolves, the pack's massive blacksmith filled up the doorway. A boar shifter — one of the gentlest, kindest people Summer had ever met. But not now. Holy cow, not now.

"Don't let us interrupt you," Ty Hawthorne growled as the five of them stood there, bristling. Sending a clear statement that the most powerful pack in the Southwest would keep a close eye on Hope Springs pack.

Summer trembled, and hell, half the gathered crowd did, too. Were her friends from the Blue Moon Saloon nearby, too? And crap, if Thomas' announcement was not to their liking, what would they do?

Thomas seemed to be the only person in the room who didn't blink an eye. He just nodded to Ty Hawthorne and went on.

"Hope Springs pack has made a name for itself in ways no honest shifter should support."

A ripple went through the crowd, and Summer's pulse skipped. Thomas was a good guy?

He swept his powerful gaze over every shifter in the room. "Ways that should make them ashamed. Too few spoke up against the men who led a rampage against innocent shifters who'd done no wrong. Too few resisted."

Summer hung her head. And she wasn't the only one.

"Many of you, I know, disapproved of the Whytes' actions."

Gretchen glared but kept her mouth shut.

"But did you act?" Thomas asked. "Did you speak up?"

He let the question hang in the air, and the room went from quiet to painfully silent as it became clear the question wasn't rhetorical. The alpha expected an answer. Confessions.

Summer understood the need for the pack members to come clean and face their past. But, damn. Who would have the balls to speak up?

Floorboards creaked as the crowd shifted nervously on their feet. Thomas' frown grew deeper. A sparrow fluttered through the eaves, and the whisper of its wings was a roar in the silence.

"I didn't act," Summer said quietly. Well, she meant to say it quietly, but the words came out loud and clear. "I didn't speak up."

Everyone whipped around, and their eyes burned into her. The girl nobody ever noticed was suddenly on center stage.

Her knees shook. Shit.

She took a deep breath. She focused on Drew and pretended he was the only one there.

You don't have to do this, his eyes said.

Oh, but she did. She could never make a future with him if she didn't get the regrets off her chest now.

"I helped Emmett track down his victims. I helped plan his ambushes."

An older man eyed her sadly with an expression that said, *But, dear. You're so young. It wasn't your fault.*

She shook her head. "I didn't know what they were doing at first. I never asked why. I never bothered thinking about what was really going on." Her voice threatened to crack, and she cleared her throat. "Which makes me just as guilty." And Jesus, did she feel the guilt. Every day. Every night.

She looked around the room, expecting glares. But the others had either lowered their eyes to the floor or were nodding in agreement.

"I knew it couldn't go on, but all I could think of was to run away. All I could think of was myself."

Drew looked at her and shook his head. *The cubs. You saved the cubs.*

That wasn't the point. Didn't he get it?

She was about to say as much, but a strong, clear voice sounded first, filling the room. It was Lana Dixon, Ty's mate. A woman with as powerful a presence as her mate.

"You were part of stopping them. You had the courage to resist."

"Not at the beginning, I didn't."

"One person can't stop a runaway train. But one brave person can still act. And you did. What you did helped defeat the Blue Bloods."

Brave. Had Lana Dixon, kick-ass alpha she-wolf of the Twin Moon pack, just called her brave? Summer locked her knees before her legs went out from under her.

"Brave enough to be the first to speak, too," Thomas said, nodding.

Holy shit. The new alpha of a pack was making a positive example of her.

Thomas looked around the crowd with fierce eyes. "This isn't about blame. This is about coming clean. We can't concentrate on building our future if we don't face the past first." He paused while staring at each person in turn. "So, who else?"

The crowd fidgeted, but then an old man spoke. "I was against it from the beginning, but they didn't listen, and I just gave up..."

A younger wolf chimed in next, gulping hard. "If my leg hadn't been hurt, I would have gone with them on their latest attack. I wanted to be part of it. I just didn't think it through."

More and more people spoke, all of them in dull, quiet tones. Their shoulders slumped, their faces were heavily lined. Some held their tongues and kept their eyes on the ground, but Summer wasn't worried about them. They were the type to follow a strong leader, and as long as that leader wasn't a Whyte...

She glanced Mett's way, but his eyes were cast down, too. She couldn't see Gretchen behind the crowd, but really, what could Gretchen do now but hold her tongue? Her powerful brothers had been killed for their sick ideas.

When the room went quiet again, Thomas' voice boomed out. "Anyone who objects to putting that all behind us, say it now."

The silence that stretched awkwardly was the death knell of the Blue Blood movement.

"Those who directly participated in the killings are dead, and we have a future to build," Thomas said. "A future in which we concentrate on rebuilding this pack in peaceful, honest ways."

She shot a glance at Drew, who grinned at her from across the room. *It's over. It's done.*

Her knees really did buckle then, and as the visiting alphas spoke up to pledge their support for Thomas — another ritual that could take hours — Summer edged out the door.

Sunlight struck her like a physical thing, and the anxiety that had chilled her body slowly faded to a warm feeling of peace. A feeling of release.

She put her hands on her knees, closed her eyes, and replayed Drew's words.

It's over. It's done.

Summer couldn't help it. The second she folded over her knees, she cried. Shook. Sobbed. It hurt, that process of tearing herself away from so much guilt and fear — but it felt good, too. So she didn't hold her emotions back. She probably couldn't if she tried. And if anyone spotted her looking like an utter mess, who cared? It was over. Finally, it was over.

When her tears ran dry, she rubbed the last demons out of her eyes and tipped her head back to the sun. A new day. A new start. She could begin her life all over again. With Drew.

The morning air smelled fresh and hopeful, as if spring was hiding right around the corner ready to jump out and cry, *Surprise!* As if every flower in the desert was about to burst out in bloom. A hummingbird zoomed by in a flash of green and gold, and somewhere in the distance, a mourning dove cooed.

She sighed and closed her eyes again. Peace. What a priceless thing. Peace outside and peace within.

She was so lost in weary relief that she didn't immediately react to the sound of shoes scuffing the earth nearby.

"Bitch." A voice cut the still air like a knife. "What are you smiling about?"

Chapter Nine

Summer jolted, but it was too late. One strong hand pinned her arms, and another slapped over her mouth. The overpowering scent of chewing tobacco flooded her nose.

Mett. Holy shit. Mett.

"I'll give you something to smile about, bitch." He half dragged, half pushed her away from the barn.

"Hurry up," someone else grunted.

Footfalls sounded all around her. Shit, Mett wasn't alone.

As he hustled her onward, she caught fleeting glimpses of the hate-filled faces of Gretchen's sons. Gretchen's not-too-bright, bloodthirsty sons. They hadn't been among those expressing their regret at the meeting, that was for sure.

She tried digging her heels into the ground, but they just skidded along. Mett was too strong, and she was too worn out. He'd caught her at that sagging moment after weeks of forcing herself to be strong, and suddenly, she couldn't find an ounce of energy any more.

You have to, a voice hissed at the back of her mind. *You have to if you want to survive.*

She bit the hand he held over her mouth, but he just slapped her.

"Traitor." Mett dug his nails into her arms, and she cried out. "Whore. Don't make it worse for yourself."

Right, worse. What could possibly make this worse?

He forced her down the steep slope of a ravine then around one bend after another, moving out of sight and earshot of the settlement. Then he screeched to a halt and thrust her forward.

She stumbled, righted herself, then froze. There was Gretchen, right in front of her.

Yeah, that was worse, all right.

Gretchen slapped her so hard, Summer's vision blurred. Something warm and sticky trickled over her chin. Blood. Gretchen had drawn blood, which immediately excited her sons.

"Show her. Show the bitch," one of them sneered.

Gretchen backhanded her a second later, and just as Summer's head rolled back to center, Gretchen slapped her once more.

The world blurred and wobbled around her, and Summer caught glimpses of more men. Was she seeing double, or had more arrived? She blinked her vision back into focus, and shit. The numbers of Mett's gang had doubled. There were at least a dozen there now, all wearing hateful expressions that said they couldn't wait to punish her. Brutally. Mercilessly.

"We worked so hard for so long," Gretchen said, and the men nodded. "Working for the good of all shifters."

The men murmured in agreement. "Purity. Purity."

Summer's stomach turned. She'd heard it all before. She'd seen the same crazed expressions on Emmett Whyte and his gang before they set off on their last ambush.

"You think we'll let you ruin all that?" Gretchen glared. "You think we'll let some outsider tell us what to do?"

By outsider, Gretchen meant Thomas, and there it was again — the scent of a conspiracy. Gretchen had some plan for getting rid of Thomas. Maybe not immediately, but soon. That much was evident in the old woman's eyes. Gretchen would play along with Thomas while he rode his initial wave of triumph, but when the other wolf packs left and Thomas turned his back, Gretchen would strike.

"We are the true," Gretchen shouted, and the men all cheered. "We will never give up our mission. And someday, shifters of all species will revere us for keeping the bloodlines strong and pure."

Bile rose in Summer's throat. Thomas might have declared the Blue Bloods gone, but the true believers lived on. They were right here, surrounding her.

Drew, she wanted to scream. *Drew. . .*

Gretchen cackled. "Call him. Call your dirty lover now."

Summer froze. How could Gretchen know? Her heart shuddered when she realized Gretchen must have caught that one moment of indiscretion when Drew first entered the meeting and locked eyes with her. If Thomas had figured them out, Gretchen could have, too.

"Call him for help," Gretchen goaded.

Every nerve in Summer's body shouted the same order, but she bit her tongue. If she called Drew, he'd be murdered in cold blood.

"Whore. You could have had it all." Mett spat at her feet.

By having it all, he meant being his mate.

Never, her wolf vowed. *Never.*

"You are sick," she managed. "You're all sick."

"You're the sick one." Mett twisted her arm. "You had your chance to join the chosen few, but you betrayed your own kind instead." He held her from behind, standing so close, his stubble scratched her cheek. "And you will pay the price." Until then, he'd held her in place with an arm around her waist, but now he reached higher and groped her breast. "How about we remind you how good a wolf can make you feel?"

The other men snickered.

She'd never felt so dirty, so used — at least, not since the day she'd discovered Emmett had been using her to aid his attacks. And all her fear and anger came back in a flood. She would never stand meek and cowed again, even if it cost her her life.

A rush of adrenaline fueled her, and she twisted in Mett's arms. She whipped her elbow around at the same time, putting her whole body into the blow. Mett fell, screaming.

"My nose! You broke my fucking nose."

She scrambled away, staring at the blood gushing down his face. Then she whirled, ready to flee.

"Going somewhere?" One of Gretchen's sons growled, blocking her path.

She spun left, but there was no way through there, either. No opening anywhere in the ring that closed in around her.

"Get her!" Mett shouted. "Punish her!"

She turned in a slow circle, holding up her fists. But, crap. How would she ever defend herself against so many? Her hands shook. Should she feel lucky to have made them angry enough to kill her outright instead of gang-raping her?

"Be done with it," Gretchen snapped. "We've been gone for long enough. The others will notice. Just kill her. Then we'll lure out that bear."

"We'll kill that bastard, too," Mett howled.

"No!" Gretchen shouted, and all the men took a step back.

Summer gaped. Crap, she'd underestimated Gretchen. Gretchen was the one at the root of it all. She'd probably been the one feeding Victor and Emmett Whyte their sick ideas.

"Damn it, she could ruin everything I've been working for," Gretchen screeched.

Summer stared. *I?* Not *we?* Then she saw the pride, the cockiness in Gretchen's eyes.

It *was* Gretchen. It had been Gretchen all along.

"We need to set the bear up first," the older woman said. "Make it look like he killed Summer out of jealousy when he found out this bitch chose Mett over him."

"Never," Summer sputtered. She wouldn't choose Mett for her life.

The men started rumbling about the details, which shifted their focus from her.

Now! her wolf barked. *This is our chance. Run!*

She spun and pushed between two men, making a break for it.

"Hey!" one shouted.

The other grabbed for her, but she darted forward just in time.

"Get her! Run!"

Oh, she'd run, all right. Summer ran like she'd never run before, pumping her arms, denying herself a glance back.

Gravel scraped as the men took up the chase. Her mind spun. How far was it back to the settlement? Could she possibly outrun these men?

Let me out, her wolf cried. *We're faster on four feet.*

True, but shifting would slow her down for a split second. Did she have enough of a lead?

The air whooshed behind her as the nearest man grabbed for her shirt. He was close. Too close to escape for long.

Then fight. Fight for your life. If they use dirty tactics, we can too, her wolf barked.

She ran up the first part of the slope then whipped around and kicked as hard as she could, sending the nearest man tumbling against the others.

Now, run. Run!

She ran, and when the slope grew steeper, she clawed at the scree with her hands and feet. She crested the ridge ahead of the men, raced around a corner—

—and smashed right into a wall of rock.

Whoa. She blinked as two arms steadied her. Make that a wall of muscle, not rock.

"Summer," the wall murmured, setting her back on her feet.

Drew. It was Drew. She would have thrown herself into a hug if it weren't for the footsteps rushing up from behind.

"Summer," he said again, but this time, it was a rumble of warning.

She stared, because she'd never seen Drew red with anger. She'd never seen his eyes flash with such hate. This was a different Drew — and yet the same, because the side of him that brushed her body was gentle and warm. Protective.

He pushed her behind the shelter of his body as Gretchen's gang stopped short in front of them.

"You," Mett hissed in a voice full of poison.

Drew didn't say anything. He only growled. So low and deep, it could have been thunder from over the hills.

Everyone froze, but the air crackled with energy. The air around Drew shimmered the way heat shimmered over a highway, signaling a shift. His growl dropped an octave. His shirt split down his back as he tipped forward onto all fours. One second, he was human, and the next, a giant black bear stood at her side.

A massive bear whose coat shook with fury as he reared up on his hind legs, looming over her.

Make that protecting her. The looming effect was intended for the others. And damn, it seemed to work, because Mett and his cousins stood perfectly still, teetering on the razor's edge between panic and testosterone-fueled instinct to fight.

Drew bared huge teeth, spread paws as big as baseball mitts, each flashing with six-inch claws, and roared.

Try me, that roar said. *Try me.*

Chapter Ten

Drew sucked in a deep breath as the wolves before him shifted and growled.

Fight with your head, not with your heart. That's what his father had always said. And he'd always listened.

But now... His whole body shook with rage, and power flowed through him the way it flowed through mighty rivers or in explosive bursts of wind. The way thunderclouds flowed over mountain ridges and swept over a valley, drowning it.

He flexed one paw then the other. This was a fight like no other, and hell yeah, he was going to fight with his heart. How could he not? This was for Summer.

Summer, who was all heart and soul.

"Drew," she said, putting a hand on the coarse fur of his back. And hell, if that didn't prove how gutsy she was, what did? She'd never seen him in bear form before, and even his own kind backed away when he stepped into battle mode.

The river of power pulsed harder, and he unleashed another roar.

You will not hurt my woman. You will die.

He hadn't done a lot of killing in his life, and he had certainly never relished it. But he'd never been so provoked, either, so blind with rage.

Summer. They wanted to kill Summer.

He roared again, and two of the wolves tucked their tails between their legs, ready to flee.

"Hold your ground, idiots." If the woman who came up behind them had been holding a whip, he'd bet anything she'd have cracked it at them. "Get him."

The wolves snarled and spread out, trying to outflank him. And shit, there was nothing to back up against to keep Summer out of harm's way. No rocky outcrop, no tree. No buildings. Just gently sloping hills that didn't help one bit.

He sidestepped one way then the other, trying to keep them all in sight. A dozen wolves against one bear. If only he had some backup — but he'd left the meeting without a word, hoping to catch up with Summer and celebrate. But, crap. There wasn't much to celebrate — other than the fact that he'd sensed her cry for help and arrived before they killed her.

"You have backup, all right," Summer said, reading his mind. She sounded fiercer than ever. She looked it, too — even more fierce and determined than when she'd spoken up in the meeting.

Run, Summer. Run. He insisted. *Get someplace safe.*

She shook her head in a vehement no. *I'm not leaving you. I'll never leave you.*

Her deep brown eyes locked on his, and the wave of power inside him surged.

I love you, she said.

It should have been an occasion for him to dance and sing. Instead, he whispered, *I love you,* then whipped his head around and roared.

A wolf leaped at him, setting off the fight, and everything was a blur from there. Growls exploded, filling the gully, and the rushing sound of scattering gravel came from all sides.

He battered an oncoming wolf with one outstretched paw and dashed it to the ground. Then he turned and shouldered two more aside.

Drew! Watch out! A deeper version of Summer's voice filled his mind. She'd shifted too and stood her ground at his side.

Another wolf barreled out of nowhere, jaws spread wide, aiming for his neck. Drew backed up quickly and swatted it aside. But that left Summer exposed, and two wolves leaped at her.

"Get her! Get her!" that witch, Gretchen, cried.

His vision went red as he hurried forward to help, and a moment later, two wolves were flying through the air. One landed against a rock and went limp, while the other rolled to its feet and scurried out of range. Summer snarled and snapped at yet another wolf who'd been sneaking up on Drew from behind.

Blood pounded in his ears as the rest of the wolves surged forward, attacking from every direction at the same time. He clawed the two in front of him, but another two landed on his back and made him stumble. Their teeth sank into his flesh, making him roar in fury.

Drew!

He couldn't tell whether Summer was shouting for help or in alarm. He swiped at his own back then rolled, crushing his attackers and following up with his fangs. Bone snapped, blood flowed, and the wolves yelped in pain.

Serves you right, he wanted to shout as he lumbered back to his feet. He raked his claws against the nearest wolf, leaving a wound not even a shifter could recover from.

Drew!

Another wolf darted forward, nipping at Drew's haunches as he looked for Summer. She was on her hind legs, clawing wildly at a wolf who attacked from the front. Her side was stained red, and her lips pulled back as she snarled and snapped. Another wolf closed in on her from behind.

No way. Not on his watch.

Drew had never moved so fast nor felt such fury. With one vicious swipe, he sent one wolf tumbling. Thank goodness Summer scrambled out of the way, because momentum carried Drew right over the second wolf, nearly crushing Summer.

A gunshot split the air, and everyone jolted. Including him. And Summer. And whoa — even the wolves.

For a split second, the fight paused.

"Keep him right there," Gretchen sneered, feeding a bullet into the chamber of an old-fashioned six-shooter.

The sun glinted off silver, and Drew's blood ran cold. Gretchen was loading silver bullets. Gretchen wanted to kill his mate.

Summer's snarl turned to a yelp of alarm. The wolves backed off, forming a barrier between him and Gretchen to buy their leader time. Every snarl, every bark said, *Now what, bear? Now what are you going to do?*

He couldn't beat a silver bullet. No shifter could. But he wasn't beaten yet.

Run, Summer! Get away! His mental shout wasn't a request. It was an order. The only order he'd ever throw his mate's way, because it meant her life. He launched himself at the wolves, determined to bust through. Even if Gretchen shot him, it would give Summer time to flee.

No, Drew. Please! Summer cried.

"Stop!" a voice boomed from the right. A human voice. Someone else was joining the fray. Thomas, maybe?

Drew didn't stop to look, because Gretchen was raising the barrel and taking aim at Summer.

No! he roared, plunging forward toward the wolves. One scrambled backward and tumbled right into Gretchen, who went sprawling.

"You fool!"

Pfft! An arrow sliced through the air where Gretchen had just stood, but with its target gone, the arrow clattered off a rock.

Drew pushed forward, fighting the weight of three wolves who'd jumped on his back in a desperate assault. Gretchen reached for her fallen gun. Shit, he had to stop her. But his steps were too slow. Sharp wolf teeth sliced into his flesh, and he bellowed in frustration.

No. He could not fail. Not now.

He pushed forward, steamrolling over a wolf. His ear burned where one of the beasts practically hung from it, trying to pull him down.

"Gretchen, no!" Thomas boomed in a clear alpha order. "Stop!"

His stern voice was enough to make her followers hesitate, but not Gretchen. Her fingers closed around the gun.

"Stop me," she sneered.

Drew! Summer cried from far too close.

He couldn't turn to face her. All he could do was chuff, urging her to get away while he plowed on. More wolves piled on him in a coordinated tackle, making him feel mired in mud.

Pfft! Another arrow whizzed by, and a wolf screamed then fell.

The archer had to be Rae — a Twin Moon she-wolf. No other shifter carried a bow, let alone shot silver-tipped arrows. Which meant Thomas wasn't the only one trying to stop the fight. If the Twin Moon wolves had arrived on the scene, too...

His hopes rose, then fell. It didn't matter who had come to help. Gretchen had silver-tipped projectiles of her own, which meant she could take down the mightiest wolf and the fiercest warrior.

He shook himself free of the pileup and raced toward Gretchen, who was raising the barrel toward Thomas.

"You think you can just waltz into this pack and change everything?" she screamed. "You think our cause can be stamped out?"

Drew snorted. He was the one with a just cause, and Gretchen was only four steps away. But, shit, she'd spotted him and was whipping around.

Bang! She let off a wild shot that whistled past his ear.

Her eyes went wide, and Christ, he bet his did, too. But he sure as hell wasn't stopping. Even if she pumped a bullet or two into him, he'd get her with his dying breath.

Must kill her. He burned the thought into every muscle, determined to see this through. He had to put an end to the Blue Blood madness once and for all. If Gretchen fell, her followers would be defeated. None of them were plotters or thinkers — not Mett, and definitely none of her sons. Without their leader, they'd be lost.

Growls sounded behind him, and he could sense the Twin Moon wolves barreling in. An arrow zipped through the air, taking out another of the rogues, and he realized he was blocking Rae's shot at Gretchen. Well, fine. If he somehow failed, the Huntress could finish Gretchen off. That arrow, meanwhile, took out another wolf.

Fine with him — one less obstacle in his path.

Gretchen's hands shook with rage as she cocked the gun and aimed.

He held his breath but forced his legs to carry on. Two more steps and he'd have Gretchen. It didn't matter that he could see down the barrel of the gun. All that mattered was protecting Summer.

Summer. Oh, how he wished he could hold her one more time. He wished fate came with a pause button to give him the chance to say good-bye. To look in her eyes and get it all out at last.

Summer, I love you. I wanted to spend my life with you.

His bear mourned the thought of losing all that — all the things he never even knew he wanted until he'd met her — but he couldn't stop now. He couldn't fail.

Drew! Summer yelped, and whoa. Why was she so close? He could sense her right over his shoulder. His job was to save her, not the other way around.

But with half a dozen grown wolves hanging from his coat, he had to admit he didn't exactly have a foolproof plan.

Gretchen's eyes narrowed as she clamped down on the trigger. His heart thumped harder, and then time stood still.

He saw the next minute play out in slow motion before it happened in real time, as if fate was giving him a preview of what was about to occur. Like an out-of-body experience before he was even dead.

The bullet would hit him right between the eyes, and he'd drop to the ground an inch short of reaching Gretchen. Summer would race in a moment later, and Gretchen would get another shot off. A wild shot that would strike Summer.

He wanted to scream and wipe the image away, but it hung in front of him, showing Summer's eyes go wide in pain then regret as the life seeped out of her.

No. No. No! That couldn't happen. He had to save her.

You can save her, a voice boomed in his head. A deep, earthy voice, like a spirit from times long past. *But not with misplaced heroics. There is another way.*

He'd have growled at whoever it was that dared doubt him, but shit — what if that was fate, speaking to him?

The bubble of time he was caught in stretched out for another heartbeat, close to bursting, and the voice in his head growled again.

Listen to me, bear. That evil woman has killed enough. There is another way.

What other way? What the hell could he do?

He replayed the scene in his mind, frantic for some clue, some idea. The wolf clinging to his left shoulder was Mett — he could tell from the tobacco-scented breath. But if he dropped his shoulder at exactly the right second...

His focus snapped back to Gretchen, and he saw the bullet shoot out of the barrel, coming straight for him. The silver tip spiraled in slow motion, but he had the feeling fate was about to hit the fast-forward switch.

Last chance, bear, the voice warned.

Every bone in his body rebelled at the idea of dodging that bullet. That was the coward's way, and he was no coward.

Prove it, then, fate challenged him. *Prove it to me.*

He wanted to shake his head and insist that facing death was the hard part. That anything could go wrong if he flung himself out of the way.

The hard part is trusting, fate boomed.

Drew! Summer's voice sounded faint, like she was a thousand miles away. *Duck! Get out of the way!*

Trust, fate murmured. *Trust.*

Drew! Summer's voice echoed in his ears, and a thousand images flashed through his mind. Images of him and her, walking hand in hand in a sun-kissed valley overflowing with wild flowers. Of Summer looking at him and laughing, then turning to look back.

Come on, she smiled, patting her knees.

He looked back and froze at the image of an unsteady toddler, reaching for Summer's hand.

Go to Daddy, Summer cheered the child along. *You can do it.*

He was seeing the future. Carefree, happy times

Last chance, bear, fate whispered and slid away.

And just like that, he was in real time again, with a bullet speeding his way.

He flung himself to the right as an explosion deafened both ears. His shoulder hit the ground, and pain blinded him. But the death cry that split the air wasn't his.

That was Mett, who grunted and fell.

Drew forced himself to roll, knocking out three wolves, and Gretchen's startled eyes followed the motion.

"You!" she hissed, tracking him with the gun.

Shoot me, he roared. *Shoot me now.*

No, he didn't have a death wish. He had a vision. If he could keep Gretchen distracted for a second longer...

A light-colored, agile wolf sprung through the air beside him. It was Summer, launching herself at Gretchen.

Trust, he reminded himself, gritting his teeth. He hated letting his mate jump into danger, but he had to do it. He had to trust fate.

Shoot me, he roared again, keeping the enemy's focus on him.

A ferocious growl split the air, and Gretchen jerked around, too late. Summer knocked her over, and the gun went flying again. Both women rolled when they struck the ground, but Summer was faster to rise to her feet. She snarled at Gretchen, facing her down.

Then, *Pfft!* Another arrow sliced through the air, and Gretchen lurched forward in wide-eyed surprise.

Summer backed away, watching Gretchen die, and in the hush that fell over the gully, Drew dashed forward, protecting his mate. He whirled, panting wildly, looking around.

There were only five rogues left standing, but Thomas leaped and took out one. A massive, dark-furred wolf ripped out the throat of another, and a lanky she-wolf wrestled a third to the ground, clamping her jaws around his neck. The biggest coyote Drew had ever seen clawed another rogue, and a huge boar steamrolled the rogue who was trying to flee, crushing it under his hooves. A cloud of dust rose, veiling the scene, and Drew backed Summer up, intent on keeping her safe.

Safe. Holy shit. Were they finally safe? He circled her three times, keeping her close. Mett's gang was all dead. But, shit. Summer was bloody and cut and—

Drew, I'm fine, she insisted, sniffing him back.

You're wounded.

Nothing serious. Nothing like you. Are you okay?

What did it matter if he was okay? He needed *her* to be okay. He turned another tight circle, keeping her safe.

The wolves that had raced to their aid coughed as the dust settled, and everyone looked around, surveying the scene.

"Whoa," Thomas said, shifting back to human form.

Safe. They were finally safe. Or were they? Drew snarled at the new alpha of Hope Springs when he stepped closer.

Thomas threw his hands up. "Is she okay?"

Genuine concern poured from his voice, and something in Drew clicked. Thomas cared for Summer? A wave of jealousy flooded over him, and he puffed out his fur, keeping Summer concealed as best he could. Yes, it was childish. Yes, he ought to trust that fate wanted him and Summer together and not Summer and some other jerk. But damn it, he wasn't risking anything.

Drew, she murmured, sticking her wolf muzzle clear of his fur. Her body pressed against his, reassuring him. *I'm okay. Everything is okay.*

He was still panting a mile a minute, and his sides heaved, but he couldn't settle down. Everything was not okay. A pack of rogues had just attacked his mate, and she'd had to dodge a silver bullet. On top of that, the newly minted pack alpha seemed to be after his woman. So, no. Nothing about this was okay, except the fact that he and Summer were still on their feet. And crap, he might not be there for long, because wounds he hadn't felt until now were suddenly announcing themselves in a dozen places that burned and ached.

Thomas held out his hands and spoke quietly. "I don't want to fight you." His eyes slid to Summer, saying, *I want to love her.*

Drew growled until Thomas took a long breath and stepped back. "Just checking she's okay," he murmured, looking sadder than a man on the cusp of a pivotal victory ought to be. "Just checking."

Checking or plotting? Drew watched Thomas until he saw the man's shoulders slump slightly.

She's yours, Thomas admitted, shooting the thought into Drew's mind. *I see that. I respect that.* He shot Summer a wry smile, then looked at Drew again. *Lucky bastard. Make sure you appreciate what you have.*

Oh, he'd appreciate it, all right. He'd cherish his mate every day for the rest of his life.

With a sigh, Thomas turned away, convincing Drew he meant it. Maybe Thomas was a man of honor, after all. Drew chuffed, and the wolf looked back.

Good luck, Drew called, feeling doubly lucky. He was the one who got the girl. All Thomas got was a mess of a pack.

Thomas nodded, standing tall to address the Twin Moon wolves. "Thanks for coming. You got my message?"

Drew gaped. It was Thomas who'd sent the anonymous message? Thomas was one of the good guys all along?

Ty Hawthorne, still in wolf form, nodded in a way that made Drew suspect there'd been further exchanges since he'd left Arizona. The dark-haired Arizona alpha paused to sniff and nuzzle his mate, then turned and walked beside Thomas, heading back to the settlement, obviously ready to discuss business.

Well, Drew wanted no part of that. All he wanted was Summer. And maybe a bed because, hell, everything hurt.

He settled for dropping to the ground. His mate was all right. Thank God for that.

Of course she is, his bear mumbled, fading slowly away. *Did you see her move?*

A smile spread over his face. Yeah, he'd seen her move, all right. All lithe and agile and graceful despite the carnage of it all.

Drew, she whispered, licking his nose with her long, wolf tongue.

She whimpered and nuzzled him and fussed over his wounds, somehow managing to make him float away on cloud nine instead of obsessing about the throbbing pain.

He broke into what had to be a goofy grin, and she did, too. *Love you, my bear.*

He sighed. *Love you, my wolf.*

It's over. It's finally over, Summer said.

He looked deep into her eyes and saw the future again. *No. It's only just the start. Our start.*

Epilogue

The bell over the door to the Quarter Moon Café chimed merrily, and three big men filed in. Summer looked up with a smile. She'd started work early, as always, forcing herself away from her slumbering mate to help Jessica bake. Leaving Drew was the hardest part of her day, which said a lot about how wonderful her life had become. She had the best job, the best home, the best mate in the world.

Her heart skipped in anticipation, hoping Drew would be among them. She'd probably never get over the excitement of seeing her mate, even if they'd only been apart for an hour or two.

"Morning, Summer." Luke tipped his hat. "Merry almost-Christmas."

The holiday was only a few days away, and she couldn't wait.

"Heya, Summer. Looks like you brought the weather with you again." Mack waved to the clear Arizona sky filling up the upper portion of the windows with a rich, vibrant blue.

"Hi, sweetheart. Gonna need some coffee to jump start my day," Sam said.

"Hi, guys." She smiled and tried not to crane her neck to see behind them.

Then a fourth man crowded the doorway, and her smile stretched cheek to cheek. Her wolf wagged its tail and cheered.

Mate! My mate!

Their eyes locked, and his smile went from happy to blissed-out with lovestruck joy.

Hers, too.

Drew stepped slowly over the threshold, rubbing a shoulder against the doorframe in a way that said, *Mine. Mine to cherish and protect.*

And it was his, in a way, just as the place was hers, too. When they'd come back from Utah, Soren and the others had invited them to join the Blue Moon clan, and she'd shed tears of joy.

I think that means yes, Drew had said, grinning a mile wide.

All she could do was nod and blubber, unable to express it all. Home. She had a real home with an honest group of shifters she loved and respected. And best of all, with her mate.

She got a permanent job working shifts in the café and saloon, and Drew did, too. He shared bartending duties in the saloon, helped out in the café at its busiest times, and did all the odd jobs Soren and Simon didn't have time to do. Which there were a hell of a lot of because both businesses were booming. The clan was flourishing, too. Jessica hadn't said anything yet, but Summer was pretty sure that new, rosy glow on her boss' cheeks didn't just come from the prospect of a little time off now that there were more hands to share the load. She'd bet anything Jess was expecting, though she didn't say a word. That was for Jessica to announce when she and Simon were ready.

Babies. Mates. Bright futures. A dozen sunny possibilities rushed through her mind as she watched Drew come through the door.

He paused and wiped his boots — such a polite bear — in that right-left, right-left pattern she knew so well and finally stepped up to her. Right up to her, nice and close.

"Morning." His green-gold eyes sparkled and danced with joy.

"Morning," she replied, trying not to blush. Because it had been a good morning. A damn good one when she'd woken naked and draped across his body with her head pillowed on his mile-wide chest. The best morning ever, it seemed like, because she was at his side.

He was so close she could kiss him, but just when she was about to, he took a tiny, teasing step back. That was a little habit he'd kept from their early days. Close-closer-back and then close again. She loved it — that reminder of how much they'd stood to lose, and how much they'd gained.

Mate, he rumbled, closing the gap again to kiss her at last.

She closed her eyes and drank in his kiss. And drank and drank as he backed her up to the wall. He held her there, his big, hard body flush against hers, and kissed her like they'd been apart for months, not hours. He nipped her lips, then smoothed them over with his tongue, and tasted her again and again.

"There they go again," Luke sighed.

"Didn't you give these kids a place to play house?" Mack joked.

"Love," Sam said. "True love. Don't mess with it, boys."

A rumbling sound came from Drew's chest, agreeing with Sam. *Don't mess with me or my mate.*

Summer reveled in his kiss for another minute before forcing herself to break it off. Because, oops, she was supposed to be working. She got as far as tucking her face against Drew's shoulder but got stuck there. Man, did he smell good. Felt good, too.

Mate. Want my mate, her wolf growled. *Don't want to wait any more.*

That was the issue — the waiting. When they'd returned to Arizona, they'd decided not to exchange mating bites until things had settled down a bit. Drew still needed some time to heal from his wounds, and she needed time to get used to feeling...well, free. Free of the crushing guilt, the need to prove herself constantly.

Believe me, he's ready, her wolf growled. *And I am, too.*

She was beginning to think they'd put off mating bites a little too long, given the way they nearly devoured each other every time they touched. A little PDA was okay, but too much...

"You know what?" Mack announced so decisively, everyone turned.

"What?" Luke replied on cue.

Mack stepped behind the counter. "I can get my own muffin, and Sam can get his own coffee. You don't mind, do you, Jess?"

Jessica grinned. "Don't mind at all."

Luke looked at Summer and Drew and jerked his head toward the back door. "Which means you two can, um..."

"Tear each other's clothes off and go at it," Mack finished. "In private, I mean. Get that mating bite on her, Drew. Please. Put us out of our misery."

Summer's cheeks burned from a blush that had to be bright red. Had they been that bad?

Jessica smiled. "Good idea. Why don't you take the rest of the morning off?"

A blush spread under Drew's dark beard, giving him a little-boy-in-a-man's-body look that made him unbearably attractive.

Well, get moving already, her wolf yowled.

"Um, well..." she stuttered, lacing her fingers through Drew's.

Mack swung his muffin plate toward the back door. "Move it, bear, and let us eat our breakfast in peace."

His words seemed to break the spell, because the next thing she knew, Drew was hurrying her out the back door.

"Ah. True love." Sam's voice sounded from behind.

"True love," she agreed, rushing along at her mate's side.

"Fate," Drew murmured. "Thank goodness for fate."

He led her across the lot and up the stairs toward the little apartment above the garage they'd moved in to together. And every step they took unleashed a little more bottled-up desire. She shed her apron and left it draped over the tinsel at the lower end of the banister. A second later, she'd wrestled Drew's shirt off and tossed it to the right. Her shirt was next, and though she went for his jeans, Drew beat her to it by popping off her bra. Their passion was a whirlwind, a tornado, a runaway train, sweeping them along in a rush of giggles, pants, and kiss-smothered exclamations.

"True love," she whispered into his lips the second he came up for air.

"Fate," he agreed, then crushed his mouth to hers and consumed her.

They sank to the stairs, his big body covering hers, his huge hands working her breasts. Then he ducked his head and kissed his way to her left nipple. The one closest to her heart.

The second his soft lips closed around the tight bud, she arched right off the stairs and into thin air. Well, it felt like it anyway. Like floating or riding a wave with Drew wrapped around her like a life jacket. She clung to him and scratched at his bare shoulders, as desperate as he was to complete their connection. Not just with kisses. Not just with another round of sex. Nothing would satisfy her until they'd exchanged mating bites.

He sucked in her nipple, released it, and smoothed it over with his tongue. "So beautiful. So perfect."

She'd never felt like either before, but Drew made her into a goddess. She really did feel beautiful and perfect.

And hungry. God, was she ravenous for her mate.

Need him inside me. Need to feel his bite, her wolf yowled.

She got his jeans off but not his boxers because he got to her pants first. It took a bit of wiggling, but a second later, her jeans and panties hung on the rail, too, a few more pieces of flotsam tossed up by the storm they created.

"Mine," he growled, and his eyes glowed. He slid a hand down her belly, over her mound, and between her legs.

Her hips lifted straight off the stairs to meet his warm, sure hand, and he slipped right in, spreading her slickness left and right.

"Drew," she moaned, reaching for his cock. His erection practically bobbed into her hand, and she wrapped her fingers around it. He was hard for her. Hard and huge.

For her. She did that to him. She turned on her mate.

Of course, we do, her wolf chuckled. *Look at him.*

His eyes had gone to half-mast, and his mouth opened in a silent exclamation an inch above her breast. The movements of his fingers slowed inside her, then quickened to match her long strokes over his cock.

Up and down, she went.

In and out. He mirrored her.

She circled the broad tip of his cock.

He circled her sex in smooth circles.

She watched him in wide-eyed delight.

His eyes closed, his head tilted, and his lips moved in silent cries of *Mine* and *Mate*.

"Oh, Drew." She'd never needed a man so badly. She'd never needed *anything* so badly. Not food. Not water. Not air. "I need you inside me."

"I am inside you," he teased, pumping his fingers deeper, making her cry out.

She squirmed in ecstasy under him, then got herself together just enough to stroke his cock.

"This," she moaned. "I need this."

She'd seen bonfires. Big ones that shot huge, swirling flames up toward the stars. And there was always a point when she thought the bonfire couldn't blaze higher, until a huge lick of flame sparked up and rose above the rest, proving her wrong. It was just like that now. And damn, *she* was that bonfire. Because she managed to arch up under Drew's bulk, push him, and work his boxers down to his knees. The head of his cock stood stiff and proud, glistening with his need.

"I need this," she insisted.

His eyes flashed, and a second later, he shed his boxers completely, picked her up, and hustled her up the remaining stairs. He paused at the top landing, though, and his dirty thoughts reached her mind.

He could set her down right there. He could spread her legs, position himself on a lower step, and lick her straight to heaven.

And boy, was that tempting. Incredibly tempting. But nothing would satisfy her right now but his cock, buried deep inside her, followed by the heat of his breath on her neck as he prepared to mark her as his.

She pushed that image into his mind, added all kinds of dirty details she didn't have words for, and watched his eyes glow brighter.

"On second thought," he murmured, rushing her to the bedroom.

The short trip was a blur, though her eyes caught one thing. The framed needlepoint on the wall of their tiny living room that said, *Home is where the heart is.* And damn, she couldn't agree more.

The moment her back hit the mattress, he was upon her, his cock notched at her entrance. He took a deep breath and paused. What was he waiting for? She searched his face.

He rested his elbows on the mattress, coming face-to-face with her. A moment of calm in the eye of the hurricane.

"I love you." He smoothed her hair back so gently, so softly, she could have cried.

"I love you." She bit her lip, worried those three words didn't capture what she really felt. Lots of people said them, but did their hearts feel too big for their chests when they did? Did their souls sing and dance the way hers did?

He kissed her — one slow kiss after so many frenzied others — telling her he didn't need words to understand what she meant.

"I love you," she repeated, a little steadier this time. "And I will die if you don't screw me through this mattress right now."

He laughed, and a dozen happy folds lined his eyes and mouth, emphasizing his huge grin.

"Got it. Got it."

He pushed back up off his elbows, and a second later, he was all serious again. All hard, all ready.

This is it, his eyes said.

This is it. She wrapped her legs around him.

He rolled his hips, and his cock slid in.

She moaned in a mixture of satisfaction and raging need then pulled her legs higher along his sides. "More. Need more."

He pulled out, thrust in again, and slowly built momentum. His first few strokes were shallow, helping her adjust. The next were deeper, less patient. And what followed — that was off the charts.

She cried out, greeting each hard, hot slide with an inner squeeze. Relishing the friction, the drag. Almost wishing she wasn't so slick, just to maximize the feeling of his skin dragging over her inner walls.

His eyes had drifted out of focus while he moved, but they snapped open then. *Maximize?*

Oops. Had she thought it clearly enough for him to catch? *I'll show you maximize,* the spark in his eyes said.

He rose to his knees, hauling her hips with him, keeping the connection. And then he started to move again. To pump. To thrust. Holding her body tight against his, not letting the slightest gap separate them.

"Yes... Yes... Yes..." she cried as he hit her deepest, most secret spots.

Drew didn't utter a word, but the glow in his eyes intensified. The steady rhythm quickened, and he grunted quietly with each pistoning move.

"Yes..." she cried, clawing at his back, trying to find an outlet for the exquisite pressure building inside. "Drew..."

His face grew even more intent as his body jackhammered against hers, moving with power and precision, hitting her G-spot again and again.

She couldn't see. She couldn't think. She couldn't speak other than calling his name. The wave had gathered under her and was lifting her up, ready to send her flying.

"Please..."

"So good," he moaned. Sweat shone all over his chest, highlighting every ridge of muscle in the midday light. "So good."

She reached her hands over her head to grip the headboard, and his eyes flickered in approval. Using her last ounce of energy, she slammed her hips upward, meeting each thrust.

"Yes... Yes..."

He mouthed the word; she cried hoarsely as they both approached the crest of the wave.

Drew's lips pulled back, and the points of his canines grew. Just the sight revved her lust up another notch.

"Yes," she urged him through his last, hard thrusts.

His eyes dropped to her neck even as his hips continued to move.

"Mate," she whispered. "Do it. I want it. I want you to bite."

Instinct shoved aside reason, guiding her body. She tipped her head back, seducing him with her pale skin.

He groaned aloud, either at the sight of her ready for him or from the building climax inside.

"Ready?" he croaked.

Did he have to ask?

He slammed into her once more. A second time, making her dizzy with ecstasy. Grunting softly, he hammered into her a third time, bottoming out and exploding inside her.

"Oh, yes..." he murmured.

She could feel his slick heat and every blissed-out emotion whirling through his mind.

And just as that high reached its tipping point, he buried his teeth in her neck and launched them both into an even greater rush.

Her vision filled with brilliant white light, her every muscle tensed, milking Drew hard. Her body burned gloriously in the two places he'd penetrated — where his cock was buried deep, deep inside her, and at the points of his teeth, gripping her neck. It wasn't a tearing, raging bite. It was the careful hold of a lover. A promise. A vow. She could feel her own pulse beat wildly as he held her, letting their souls connect.

Everything faded away, even the boundaries between their bodies, until all she sensed was heat — heat and joy, filling her up. Her hands might have been gripping the headboard, Drew's shoulders, or thin air. She didn't know. Didn't care. All she wanted was to hold on to the moment forever.

So she did. At least, it felt like forever — the best kind of forever. Even when the world crept back into focus and she became aware of Drew panting wildly beside her, completely spent, the pleasure stretched on and on and on.

The best part is, it's not just a one-time deal, Jessica had once told her with a naughty look. *Once you're mated, you can bite as often as you like.*

She took a deep breath. Holy Toledo, she'd never had sex like that.

Not done yet, her wolf yowled, demanding its turn.

She ran her hands over Drew's chest and slowly, slowly stretched out across his body.

"Bliss," she murmured.

He squeezed her against his chest and kissed her forehead.

Neck. Bite. Mate, her wolf barked.

She slid into a straddle, and his eyes flashed.

"Not too worn out for a little more?" she teased.

He guided her lower to his already hardening cock. "Ready. And not just for a little more."

The heat swirled out of nowhere, like embers hiding under the ashes of a forest fire, kindled by a fateful wind. And just like that, she was ablaze again.

She sat up and sank onto him, groaning with the sensation of being filled again. And on instinct, her hips began to rock.

She leaned back, riding him harder and harder. He reached up to cup her breasts, to tease her clit, making her crazy with need.

"Drew..."

Her orgasm was already rushing up to the surface. Were her eyes glowing as brightly as his?

He gulped and tipped his head back. The mighty bear, welcoming her bite. His hands squeezed her hips tightly, and he thrust up.

She arched back, groaning, and her canines extended from her gums.

My turn, her wolf demanded. *My turn.*

She bucked over him, about to lose control. Drew came inside her, and she shuddered with pleasure, unable to hold back any more. Everything was the heat, the ache, the burning need to complete the ritual. The room was blurry, the air crackled with energy. Instinct guided her to his neck, telling her exactly where it was safe to bite and how. So she did, vaguely aware of how her teeth pushed flesh and veins aside, not damaging anything but the outer layer of skin.

"Summer..."

He held her so tight to his body, her ribs ached. But that only added to the high. His thoughts echoed in her head, and a thousand images swirled through her mind. Childhood memories and beautiful sunsets and songs and delicious tastes — some from his past, some from hers. Her heart pounded in her chest, and blood rushed through her veins. Wait — his veins. She could feel the push near her teeth, but it seemed like part of her body, not his. Every part of him became part of her.

Mine! her wolf crowed. *My mate! Forever!*

Heat surrounded her like a thick blanket, and the whole room seemed fuzzy and vague.

She found herself panting and realized she'd let go. Panicked, she checked his neck, but the puncture marks from her teeth were already healing. He was all right. She was all right.

"More than all right," he whispered hoarsely, gathering her in his arms.

Her bones turned to jelly as she melted over him, settling into the curve of his body as if she'd done it all her life. Holding his shoulders, telling fate it would never force them apart.

"I don't think we have to worry about that." He smiled.

His chest was her pillow, his belly her mattress, and the ear she had pressed to his body echoed with the heavy beats of his heart. She lay there quietly, never wanting the moment to end. Then she realized it didn't really have to end. Drew was right. This was just a beginning, not an end.

She inhaled deeply, then sighed, wishing she could put it all into words.

But once again, she didn't have to.

"I know what you mean," Drew whispered, kissing her gently. "I know what you mean."

Sneak Peek: Celebration

Shifters, holidays, secret babies — ho, ho, ho!

It's been a long, hard couple of months, but the bear and wolf shifters of the Blue Moon Saloon are ready to celebrate their hard-won peace with a few days off. While some couples use the time to relax with breakfast in bed, others head out for small, intimate adventures in the desert Southwest. A few are still busy stuffing stockings and wrapping presents for little Teddy, the youngest member of the growing new clan. But Teddy won't be the only Blue Moon baby for long, because Santa has a very special surprise in store — not just for the extended Blue Moon family, but for the wolves of Twin Moon Ranch, too!

Don't miss the passion, suspense,, or romance. Get your copy of CELEBRATION today!

Books by Anna Lowe

Blue Moon Saloon

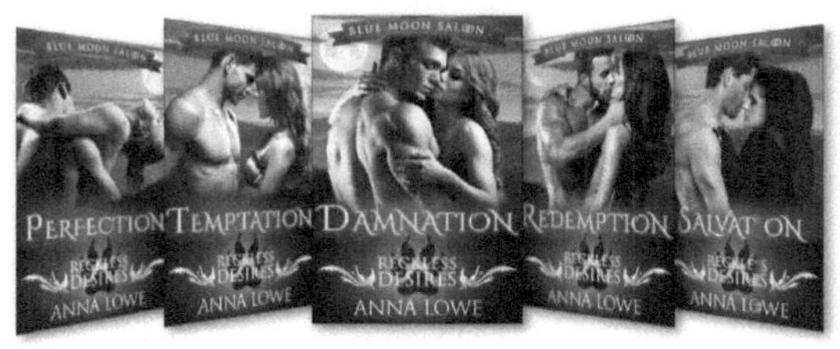

Perfection (a short story prequel)

Damnation (Book 1)

Temptation (Book 2)

Redemption (Book 3)

Salvation (Book 4)

Deception (Book 5)

Celebration (a holiday treat)

Aloha Shifters - Jewels of the Heart

Lure of the Dragon (Book 1)

Lure of the Wolf (Book 2)

Lure of the Bear (Book 3)

Lure of the Tiger (Book 4)

Love of the Dragon (Book 5)

Lure of the Fox (Book 6)

Aloha Shifters - Pearls of Desire

Rebel Dragon (Book 1)

Rebel Bear (Book 2)

Rebel Lion (Book 3)

Rebel Wolf (Book 4)

Rebel Heart (A prequel to Book 5)

Rebel Alpha (Book 5)

Fire Maidens - Billionaires & Bodyguards

Fire Maidens: Paris (Book 1)

Fire Maidens: London (Book 2)

Fire Maidens: Rome (Book 3)

Fire Maidens: Portugal (Book 4)

Fire Maidens: Ireland (Book 5)

The Wolves of Twin Moon Ranch

Desert Hunt (the Prequel)

Desert Moon (Book 1)

Desert Blood (Book 2)

Desert Fate (Book 3)

Desert Heart (Book 4)

Desert Rose (Book 5)

Desert Roots (Book 6)

Desert Yule (a short story)

Desert Wolf: Complete Collection (Four short stories)

Sasquatch Surprise (a Twin Moon spin-off story)

Shifters in Vegas

Paranormal romance with a zany twist

Gambling on Trouble

Gambling on Her Dragon

Gambling on Her Bear

Serendipity Adventure Romance

Off the Charts

Uncharted

Entangled

Windswept

Adrift

About the Author

USA Today and Amazon bestselling author Anna Lowe loves putting the "hero" back into heroine and letting location ignite a passionate romance. She likes a heroine who is independent, intelligent, and imperfect – a woman who is doing just fine on her own. But give the heroine a good man – not to mention a chance to overcome her own inhibitions – and she'll never turn down the chance for adventure, nor shy away from danger.

Anna loves dogs, sports, and travel – and letting those inspire her fiction. On any given weekend, you might find her hiking in the mountains or hunched over her laptop, working on her latest story. Either way, the day will end with a chunk of dark chocolate and a good read.

Visit AnnaLoweBooks.com